Dear Reader,

Welcome to a new and totally compelling family saga, set in the glamorous, cutthroat world of opal dealing in Australia.

Laden with dark secrets, forbidden desires, scandalous discoveries and happy endings, HEARTS OF FIRE unfolds over a series of six books, from now until December. Beautiful, innocent Gemma Smith goes in search of a new life, and fate introduces her to Nathan Whitmore, the ruthless, talented and utterly controlled screenwriter and acting head of Whitmore Opals.

Throughout the series, Gemma will discover the truth about Nathan, seduction, her real mother and the priceless Black Opal. But, at the same time, in each novel you'll find an independent, fully developed romance that can be read on its own, revealing the passion, deception and hope that has existed between two fabulously rich clans over twenty tempestuous years.

HEARTS OF FIRE has been especially written by one of romance fiction's rising stars for you to enjoy—we're sure you will.

THE EDITOR

MIRANDA LEE is Australian, living near Sydney. Born and raised in the bush, she was boarding school educated and briefly pursued a classical music career before embracing the world of computers. Happily married, with three daughters, she began writing when family commitments kept her at home. She likes to create stories that are believable, modern, fast paced and sexy. Her interests include reading meaty sagas, doing word puzzles, gambling and going to the movies.

Books by Miranda Lee

HARLEQUIN PRESENTS
1651—A DATE WITH DESTINY
1664—A DARING PROPOSITION
1702—KNIGHT TO THE RESCUE
1711—BETH AND THE BARBARIAN
1728—MARRIAGE IN JEOPARDY
1737—AN OUTRAGEOUS PROPOSAL

MIRANDA LEE

Seduction & Sacrifice

HEARTS
OF
FIRE
1

Harlequin Books

TORONTO • NEW YORK • LONDON
AMSTERDAM • PARIS • SYDNEY • HAMBURG
STOCKHOLM • ATHENS • TOKYO • MILAN
MADRID • WARSAW • BUDAPEST • AUCKLAND

ISBN 0-373-11754-X

SEDUCTION AND SACRIFICE

Copyright © 1994 by Miranda Lee.

First North American Publication 1995.

PRINCIPAL CHARACTERS IN THIS BOOK

GEMMA SMITH: on her father's death, Gemma discovers a magnificent black opal worth a small fortune and an old photograph that casts doubt on her real identity. In quest of the truth and a new life, she sets off for Sydney....

NATHAN WHITMORE: adopted son of Byron Whitmore, Nathan is acting head of Whitmore Opals and a talented screenwriter. After a troubled childhood, and a divorce, he is ruthless and utterly emotionally controlled.

LENORE LANGTRY: talented stage actress, ex-wife of Nathan Whitmore and mother of Kirsty. Lenore's tough exterior hides her unrequited love for successful solicitor, Zachary Marsden.

ZACHARY MARSDEN: married with two sons, Zachary has always been attracted to Lenore, but has so far stayed faithful to his wife.

KIRSTY WHITMORE: the wayward fourteen-year-old daughter of Nathan and Lenore has never come to terms with their divorce.

JADE WHITMORE: the spoiled, willful daughter of Byron and the late Irene Whitmore, Jade can't have the one man she wants—her adopted brother, Nathan.

BYRON WHITMORE: recently widowed, Byron is the patriarch of the Whitmore family, and a stranger to love.

MELANIE LLOYD: housekeeper to the Whitmores, Melanie is emotionally dead since the tragic deaths of her husband and only child.

AVA WHITMORE: Byron's much younger sister, Ava struggles with her weight, being unmarried and her fear of failure.

A NOTE TO THE READER:
This novel is one of a series of six. Each novel is independent and be read on its own. It is the author's suggestion, however, that the novels be read in the order written.

FAMILY TREE

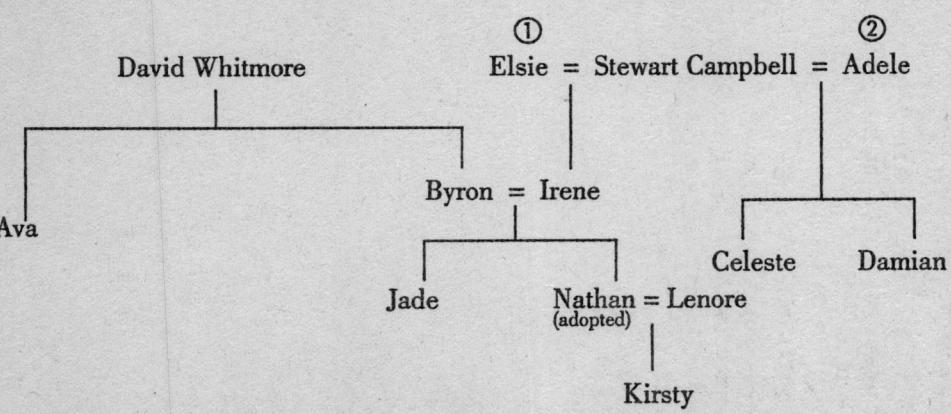

CHAPTER ONE

SHE didn't cry. Neither did anyone else attending her father's funeral.

Not that there were many mourners standing round the grave-side that hot February morning at the Lightning Ridge Cemetery. Only the minister, Mr Gunther, Ma, and Gemma herself. The undertaker had left as soon as he'd dropped off the deceased. If you stretched a point, the grave-digger made five.

Admittedly, it was forty degrees in the shade, not the sort of day one would want to stand out in the sun for more than a few minutes unless compelled to do so out of duty. Gemma watched the coffin being lowered into the ground, but still she couldn't cry.

The minister didn't take long to scuttle off, she noticed bleakly, nor did Mr Gunther, leaving her to listen to that awful sound as the clods of dirt struck the lid of the coffin.

Why can't I cry? she asked herself once more.

She jumped when Ma touched her on the shoulder. 'Come on, love. Time to go home.'

Home...

Gemma dragged in then expelled a shuddering sigh. Had she ever thought of that ghastly dugout with its primitive dunny and dirt floors as home? Yet it had been, for as long as she could remember.

'Do you want me to drive?' Ma asked as they approached the rusted-out utility truck that had belonged to Jon Smith and which was now the property of his one and only child.

Gemma smiled at Ma, who was about the worst driver she had ever encountered. Her real name was Mrs Madge Walton, but she was known as Ma to the locals. She and her husband had come to try their luck in the opal fields at Lightning Ridge more than thirty years ago. When Bill Walton died, Ma had stayed on, living in a caravan and supplementing her widow's pension by fossicking for opals and selling her finds to tourists.

She was Gemma's neighbour and had often given Gemma sanctuary when her father had been in one of his foul moods. She was the closest thing to a mother Gemma had had, her own mother having died at her birth.

'No, Ma,' she said. 'I'll drive.'

They climbed into the cabin, which was stifling despite the windows being down. Bushflies crawled all over the windscreen.

'What are you going to do now, love?' Ma asked once they were under way. 'I dare say you won't stay in Lightning Ridge. You always fancied livin' in the city, didn't you?'

There was no use lying to Ma. She knew Gemma better than anybody. 'I might go to Sydney,' she said.

'I came from Sydney, originally. Nasty place.'

'In what way?'

'Too big and too noisy.'

'I could take a bit of noise after living out here,' Gemma muttered.

'What will you do with Blue?'

Blue was Gemma's pet cattle-dog. Her father had bought him a few years back, fully grown, because he was a fierce guard-dog. He'd chained him up outside the entrance to the dugout and God help anybody who went near him. Gemma had rather enjoyed the challenge of making friends with the dog and had astounded both her father and Ma by eventually winning the animal's total loyalty and devotion. The dog adored Gemma and she adored him. She didn't have to think long over her answer to Ma's question.

'Take him with me, of course.'

'He won't like the city, love.'

'He'll like wherever I am,' Gemma said stubbornly.

'Aye, that he probably will. Never seen a dog so attached to a person. He still frightens the dickens out of me, though.'

'He's as gentle as a lamb.'

'Only with you, love. Only with you.'

Gemma laughed.

'That's better,' Ma said. 'It's good to hear you laugh again.'

Gemma fell silent. But I still haven't cried, she thought. It bothered her, very much. A daughter should cry when her father died.

She frowned and fell silent. They swept back into town and out along Three Mile Road.

Both Ma and Gemma lived a few miles out of Lightning Ridge, on the opposite side to the cemetery, near a spot called Frog Hollow. It wasn't much different from most places around the Ridge. The dry, rocky lunar landscape was pretty much the same wherever the ground had been decimated by mine shaft after mine shaft. Picturesque it was not. Nor green. The predominant colour was greyish-white.

Ma's caravan was parked under a fairly large old ironbark tree, but the lack of rainfall meant a meagre leafage which didn't provide much shade from the searing summer sun. Gemma's dugout, by comparison, was cool.

'Come and sit in my place for a while,' Gemma offered as they approached Ma's caravan. 'We'll have a cool drink together.'

'That's kind of you, love. Yes, I'd like that.'

Gemma drove on past the caravan, quickly covering the short distance between it and her father's claim. She began to frown when Blue didn't come charging down the dirt road towards her as he always did. Scrunching up her eyes against the glare of the sun, she peered ahead and thought she made out a dark shape lying in the dust in front of the dugout. It looked ominously still.

'Oh, no,' she cried, and, slamming on the brakes, she
dived out of the utility practically before it was stopped.
'Blue!' she shouted, and ran, falling to her knees in the
dirt before him and scooping his motionless form into her
lap. His head lolled to one side, a dried froth around his
lips.

'He's *dead*!' she gasped, and lifted horrified eyes to
Ma, who was looking down at the sorry sight with pity in
her big red face.

'Yes, love. It seems so.'

'But how?' she moaned. 'Why?'

'Poisoned, by the look of it.'

'Poisoned! But who would poison my Blue?'

'He wasn't a well-loved dog around here,' Ma reminded gently. 'There, there . . .' She laid a kind hand on
Gemma's shaking shoulder. 'Perhaps it's all for the best.
You couldn't have taken him to Sydney with you, you
know. With everyone but you he used to bite first and ask
questions afterwards.'

'But he was my friend,' Gemma wailed, her eyes
flooding with tears. 'I *loved* him!'

'Yes . . . yes, I know you did. I'm so sorry, love.'

The dam began to break, the one she'd been holding on
to since the police came and told her that her father had
fallen down an abandoned mine shaft and broken his
stupid damned drunken neck.

'Oh, Blue,' she sobbed, and buried her head in the
dog's dusty coat. 'Don't leave me. Please don't leave me.
I'll be all alone . . .'

'We're *all* alone, Gemma,' was Ma's weary advice.

Gemma's head shot up, brown eyes bright with tears,
her tear-stained face showing a depth of emotion she
hadn't inherited from her father. 'Don't say that, Ma.
That's terrible. Not everyone is like my father was. Most
people need other people. I know I do. And you do too.
One day, I'm going to find some really nice man and
marry him and have a whole lot of children. Not one or
two, but half a dozen, and I'm going to teach them that
the most joyous wonderful thing in this world is loving

one another and caring for one another, openly, with hugs and kisses and lots of laughter. Because I'm tired of loneliness and misery and meanness. I've had a gutful of hateful people who would poison my dog and...and...'

She couldn't go on, everything inside her chest shaking and shaking. Once again, she buried her face in her pet's already dulling coat and cried and cried.

Ma plonked down in the dirt beside her and kept patting her on the shoulder. 'You're right, love. You're right. Have a good cry, there's a good girl. You deserve it.'

When Gemma was done crying, she stood up, found a shovel and dug Blue a grave. Wrapping him in an old sheet, she placed him in the bottom of the dusty trench and filled it in, patting the dirt down with an odd feeling of finality. A chapter had closed in her life. Another was about to begin. She would not look back. She would go forward. These two deaths had set her free of the past, a past that had not always been happy. The future was hers to create. And by God, she hoped to make a better job of it than her father had of the last eighteen years.

'Well, Ma,' she said when she returned to the cool of the dugout, 'that's done.'

'Yes, love.'

'Time to make plans,' she said, and pulled up a chair opposite Ma at the wooden slab that served as a table.

'Plans?'

'Yes, plans. How would you like to buy my ute and live here while I'm away?'

'Well, I—er— How long are you going for?'

'I'm not sure. A while. Maybe forever. I'll keep you posted.'

'I'll miss you,' Ma sighed. 'But I understand. What must be must be. Besides...' She grinned her old toothless grin. 'I always had a hankerin' to live here, especially in the summer.'

'You could have your caravan moved here as well. Give you the best of both worlds. I won't sell you Dad's claim but you're welcome to anything you can find while I'm gone.'

'Sounds good to me.'

'Let's have a beer to celebrate our deal.'

'Sounds *very* good to me.'

Gemma spoke and acted with positive confidence in Ma's presence, but once she was gone, Gemma slumped across the table, her face buried in her hands. But she'd cried all the tears she was going to cry, it seemed, and soon her mind was ticking away on what money she could scrape together for her big adventure of going to Sydney.

Though a country girl of limited experience, Gemma was far from dumb or ignorant. Television at school and her classmates' more regular homes in town had given her a pretty good idea of the world outside of Lightning Ridge. She might be a slightly rough product of the outback of Australia, living all her life with a bunch of misfits and dreamers, but she had a sharp mind and a lot of common sense. Money meant safety. She would need as much as she could get her hands on if she wanted to go to Sydney.

There were nearly three hundred dollars in her bank account, saved from her casual waitressing job, the only employment she'd been able to get since leaving school three months ago. She'd been lucky to get even that. Times were very bad around the Ridge, despite several miners reportedly having struck it rich at some new rushes out around Coocoran Lake.

Then there was Ma's agreed five hundred dollars for the ute. That made just on eight hundred. But Gemma needed more to embark on such a journey. There would be her bus and train fare to pay for, then accommodation and food till she could find work. And she'd need some clothes. Eight hundred wasn't enough.

Gemma's head inevitably turned towards her father's bed against the far wall. She'd long known about the battered old biscuit tin, hidden in a hole in the dirty wall behind the headboard, but had never dared take it out to see what was in it. She'd always suspected it contained a small hoard of opals, the ones her father cashed in whenever he wanted to go on a drinking binge. It took

Gemma a few moments to accept that nothing and no one could stop her now from seeing what the failed miner had coveted so secretly.

Her heart began to pound as she drew the tin from its hiding place and brought it back to the table. Pulling up her rickety chair once more, she sat down and simply stared at it for a few moments. Logic told Gemma there couldn't be anything of great value lying within, yet her hands were trembling slightly as they forced the metal lid upwards.

What she saw in the bottom of the tin stopped her heart for a few seconds. Could it really be what it looked like? Or was it just a worthless piece of potch?

But surely her father would not hide away something worthless!

Her hand reached into the tin to curve around the grey, oval-shaped stone. It filled her palm, its size and weight making her heart thud more heavily. My God, if this was what she thought it was...

Feeling a smooth surface underneath, she drew a nobby out and turned it over, her eyes flinging wide. A section of the rough outer layer had been sliced away to reveal the opal beneath. As Gemma gently rolled the stone back and forth to see the play of colour, she realised she was looking at a small fortune. There had to be a thousand carats here at least! And the pattern was a pinfire, if she wasn't mistaken. Quite rare.

She blinked as the burst of red lights flashed out at her a second time, dazzling in their fiery beauty before changing to blue, then violet, then green, then back to that vivid glowing red.

My God, I'm rich, she thought.

But any shock or excitement quickly changed to confusion.

Her father had never made any decent strikes or finds in her various claims he'd worked over the years here at Lightning Ridge. Or at least... that was what he'd always told her. Clearly, however, he must have at some time uncovered this treasure, this pot of gold.

A fierce resentment welled up inside Gemma. There had been no need for them to live in this primitive dugout all these years, no need to be reduced to charity, as had often happened, no need to be pitied and talked about.

Shaking her head in dismay and bewilderment, she put the stone down on the table and stared blankly back into the tin. There remained maybe twenty or thirty small chunks of opals scattered in the corners, nothing worth more than ten, or maybe twenty dollars each at most. Her father's drinking money, as she'd suspected.

It was when she began idly scooping the stones over into one corner to pick them up that she noticed the photograph lying underneath. It was faded and yellowed, its edges and corners very worn as though it had been handled a lot. Momentarily distracted from her ragged emotions, she picked up the small photo to frown at the man and woman in it. Both were strangers.

But as Gemma's big brown eyes narrowed to stare at the man some more, her stomach contracted fiercely. The handsome blond giant staring back at her bore little resemblance to the bald, bedraggled, beer-bellied man she'd buried today. But his eyes were the eyes of Jon Smith— her father. They were unforgettable eyes, a very light blue, as cold and hard as arctic ice. Gemma shivered as they seemed to lock on to hers.

Her father had been a cold, hard man. She'd tried to be a good daughter to him, doing all the cooking and cleaning, putting him to bed when he came home rolling drunk, listening to his tales of misery and woe. Drink had always made him maudlin.

There were times, however, when Gemma had suspected it wasn't love that kept her tied to her father. It was probably fear. He'd slapped her more times than she could count, as well as having a way of looking at her sometimes that chilled her right through. She recalled being on the end of one of those looks a few weeks back when she'd mentioned going to Walgett to try to find work. He'd forbidden her from going anywhere, and the steely glint in his eyes had made her comply in obedient silence.

A long, shuddering sigh puffed from Gemma's lungs, making her aware how tightly she had been holding her breath. Her gaze focused back on the photograph, moving across to the woman her father was holding firmly to his side.

Gemma caught her breath once more. For the young woman appearing to resent her father's hold looked pregnant. About six months.

My God, she realised, it had to be her mother!

Gemma's heart started to race as she stared at the delicate dark-haired young woman whose body language bespoke an unwillingness to be held so closely, whose tanned slender arms were wrapped protectively around her bulging stomach, whose fingers were entwined across the mound of her unborn baby with a white-knuckled intensity.

So this was the 'slut' her father refused to speak of, who had died giving birth but who still lived within her daughter's genes. Gemma's father had told her once that she took after her mother, but other than that one snarled comment she knew nothing about the woman who'd borne her. Any curiosity about her had long been forcibly suppressed, only to burst to life now with a vengeance.

Gemma avidly studied the photograph, anxious to spot the similarities between mother and daughter. But she was disappointed to find no great resemblance, other than the dark wavy hair. Of course it was impossible to tell with the woman in the photograph wearing sunglasses. She supposed their faces were a similar shape, both being oval, and yes, they had the same pointy chin. But Gemma was taller, and much more shapely. Other than her being pregnant, this young woman had the body of a child. Or was it the shapelessness of the cheap floral dress that made her look as if she had no bust or hips?

'Mary,' Gemma whispered aloud, then frowned. Odd. She didn't look like a Mary. But that had been her name on Gemma's birth certificate. Her maiden name had been Bell and she'd been born in Sydney.

A sudden thought struck and Gemma flipped the photograph over. Written in the top left hand corner were some words. 'Stefan and Mary. Christmas, 1973'.

The date sent Gemma's head into a spin. If that was her mother in the photograph, pregnant with *her*, then she'd been born early in 1974, not September 1975! She was nearly twenty in that case, not eighteen...

Gemma was stunned, yet not for a moment did her mind refute her new age. It explained so much, really. Her shooting up in height before any other girl in her class. Her getting her periods so early, and her breasts. Then later, in high school, the way she'd always felt different from her classmates. She hadn't been different at all. She'd simply been older!

Distress enveloped Gemma as she stared, not only at the date on the photograph, but at the Stefan part. Stefan had to be her father's real name, not Jon. Lies, she realised. He'd told her nothing but lies. Why? What lay behind it all?

Gemma conceded she'd always suspected her father's name of Jon Smith might be an alias. He'd been a Swede through and through, with Nordic colouring and a thick accent. But the opal fields of outback Australia was a well-known haven for runaways, mostly criminals or married men who'd deserted their wives and families, all seeking the anonymity and relative safety of isolated places. People did not ask too many questions around Lightning Ridge, not even daughters.

But the questions were very definitely tumbling through Gemma's mind now. What other lies had her father told her? Maybe her mother *hadn't* died. Maybe she was out there somewhere, alive and well. Maybe her father had stolen her as a baby, changed his name and lied about her age to hide them both from anyone searching for them. Maybe he—

Gemma pulled herself up short. She was grasping at straws, trying to make her life fit some romantic sce-

nario like you saw on television, where a long-lost
daughter found her mother after twenty years. Life was
rarely like that. There was probably a host of reasons why
her father had changed his name, as well as her age. He'd
been a secretive man, as well as a controlling one. Maybe
he'd thought he could keep his daughter under his thumb
longer if she believed she was younger. Or maybe he'd
simply lied to authorities about her age that time when
they'd tackled him about why he hadn't sent her to school
yet.

Gemma could still remember the welfare lady coming
out here to see her father. Despite her being a little girl at
the time, and dreadfully shy, the visit had stuck in her
mind because the lady had been so pretty and smelled so
good. It was shortly after the social worker's visit that
Gemma had been sent to school. Her 'birth certificate'
had surfaced a few years later when she had wanted to
join a local netball team.

Gemma was totally absorbed in her thoughts when
suddenly the sunlight that was streaming in and on to the
table vanished, a large silhouette, filling the open doorway of the dugout. She froze for a second, then quickly
shoved the photo and opal back and snapped the lid of
the tin shut.

'Anyone home?' a familiar voice asked.

'Oh, it's only you, Ma,' Gemma said, sighing as she
stood up and walked forward across the dirt floor.

Her relief was unnervingly intense. For a split second,
she'd been afraid her unexpected visitor might have been
someone else. Which was silly, really. It had been six
years and he hadn't come near her, hadn't even spoken
to her when they'd passed on the street. There again, her
father was no longer around to act as a deterrent.

And neither was Blue, she realised with a sickening
lurch in her stomach. Oh, my God, was that who had
poisoned her dog?

'Come in and sit down, Ma,' Gemma offered, trying
to keep her steady voice while her insides were churning.
'You're just the person I need to see.'

'Really? What about?' Ma bulldozed her bulk over to the table and plonked down in a chair, which protested noisily.

'I was wondering if you'd mind if I slept in your caravan tonight. I feel a bit nervous staying here on my own.' Which was a huge understatement at this moment.

'Do you know, that's exactly what I came over here to see you about? I was thinking to myself that Gemma's too good-looking a girl to be stayin' way out here on her own. There are some none too scrupulous men living around these parts.'

Gemma shuddered, her mind whisking to one particular man, a big brute of a miner who had large gnarled hands and had always smelled of body odour and cheap whisky.

'Well, I wouldn't say I'm God's gift to men, Ma, and I could certainly lose a pound or two, but, as you say, some men aren't fussy.'

'Lose a pound or two?' Ma spluttered. 'Why, girl, have you looked at yourself in the mirror lately? Maybe a few months ago you might have had a layer of puppy fat on you, but you've trimmed down this summer to a fine figure of a woman, believe me. And you've always had the prettiest face, though you should start usin' some sunscreen on it. Mediterranean brown is all right for legs and arms but not for faces. You don't want to wrinkle up that lovely clear skin of yours, do you?'

Gemma didn't know how to take this welter of compliments. It wasn't like Ma to rave on so.

'You make it sound like I'm beautiful or something,' she protested with an embarrassed laugh.

'Or *something* just about describes it,' Ma muttered. 'You'll have to watch yourself when you get to Sydney, my girl. City men are vultures.'

'I'm not much interested in men at the moment,' Gemma replied stiffly. God, she'd thought she'd got over that other business. But she hadn't at all. It had been there lurking in the depths of her mind, waiting to be dragged up to the surface again, just as *he* had been lurking, waiting for the opportunity to assault her again.

Ma reached out to pat her on the wrist. 'Stop thinkin' about him, dear. He isn't worth thinkin' about, you know. Men like him never are.'

Gemma gaped a moment before the penny dropped. Ma wasn't talking about him. She was talking about her father. 'What do you mean by men like him?'

'Cruel. Selfish. Mean.'

The word 'mean' struck a chord with Gemma. Was that why her father hadn't sold the opal? Because he was a miser, like Scrooge? Had he gained pleasure by bringing the stone out late at night to drool over its beauty all by himself in secret?

She would never know now. That she was certain of. Jon Smith had not shared the existence of the opal with anyone, even his daughter. He'd dressed her in second-hand clothes and accepted food hand-outs rather than part with his precious prize.

Oh, yes, he'd been a mean man.

Suddenly, she was sorely tempted to show Ma the opal and ask her advice, but people had long stopped showing valuable finds around Lightning Ridge. Greed and envy did strange things to even the closest of friends. So she kept her own counsel and said, 'Yes, he was mean. But he was my father and he could have been worse.'

'You'd find excuses for Hitler,' Ma scoffed. 'How are you set for money?'

Once again, Gemma resisted the temptation to confess all to Ma. 'There's a small parcel of opals Dad saved that I can sell,' she admitted. 'Other than that I've got about twenty dollars left out of the housekeeping, three hundred dollars savings in the bank, and the money you're going to give me for the truck.'

'Which I brought over with me,' Ma said, and pulled a roll of money from the pocket of her dress. 'Don't tell the taxman but I did rather well with my fossicking this year.'

Gemma laughed. 'I won't breathe a word.'

'So when are you off to Sydney?'

A nervous lump immediately formed in Gemma's throat. My God, the furthest she'd been from Lightning Ridge was Walgett, a whole forty or so miles away. Sydney was another world, a big frightening exciting world! But wild horses wouldn't keep her away. Not now. Sydney held even more attractions than ever. Her mother had been born in Sydney. Maybe she had relatives there. Maybe she could find them.

'As soon as I can get myself organised, I suppose,' she said, her resolve deepening.

'Mr Whitmore's due in town day after tomorrow if you want to sell those opals. He'll give you a fairer price than most. Don't take his first offer, though, haggle a little.'

Gemma frowned. Her father hadn't liked Mr Whitmore for some reason, had refused to have anything to do with him, saying slick city buyers couldn't be trusted.

'Dad used to sell his opals to Mr Gunther,' she said hesitantly.

'That old skinflint? Look, I know he came to the funeral today and Jon might have been able to bully a fair price out of him, but he'll try to fleece *you* blind. You listen to me, love, and try Byron Whitmore. A fairer man never drew breath. Just go along to the Ridge Motel any time next Friday and ask for his room.'

'All right, Ma. I'll do that.'

'Good. Now you can get me a beer, love. It's bloody hot today.'

Gemma rose to get her visitor a beer. There were still several cans in the small gas fridge and a full carton leaning up against the far wall. If there was one thing her father never stinted himself on, it was beer.

'So tell me,' Gemma said on returning to the table and handing the beer over, 'what's this Mr Whitmore like?'

Ma snapped back the ring top on the can and gulped deeply before answering. 'Byron?' She wiped her mouth with the back of her hand. 'A big man. Around fifty, I'd say, but he looks younger. Thick wavy black hair sprinkled with grey and the most wonderful blue eyes. Very handsome. Too old for you, though, love. He's married as well, not that that seems to bother some men once their wives are out of sight.'

Gemma's eyes rounded and Ma gave a dry laugh. 'You are an innocent, aren't you? Better wise up before you go to Sydney. City men live fast and play fast, and they have an insatiable appetite for lovely young things with big brown eyes and bodies like yours. Still, I don't think you need worry about Byron Whitmore. He's a man of honour. A rare commodity indeed!'

Ma made Sydney sound like a huge dark forest full of big bad wolves. Surely it couldn't be as bad as that! Besides, no man would get to first base with her unless he was good and decent and kind. Maybe no man would *ever* get to first base with her, she worried anew.

That experience years ago had scarred her more than she realised. She'd thought she'd shunned boys up till now because they bored her. Now she interpreted her lack of interest in the opposite sex as a very real wariness. But was it a wariness of the boys themselves, or her own inner self, incapable perhaps of responding to a man in a normal, natural way? Dear God, she hoped that wasn't so. For if it was, how was she ever going to be happily married and have children of her own?

'Don't you believe me, love?' Ma said. 'About Mr Whitmore?'

'What? Oh, yes, Ma, I believe you. I'm sorry. I was wool-gathering.'

'You've had a long, trying day. Look, come over around six and I'll have a nice dinner ready for you. And bring your nightie.'

Gemma's eyes blurred. 'You're so good to me.'

'What rubbish! What are neighbours for?'

But Ma's faded blue eyes were a little teary too as she stood up. Gemma vowed to write to the dear old thing as often as she could from Sydney. And she would come back to visit. Often. It was the least she could do. If that black opal was worth what she thought it was worth, she'd be able to fly back in style!

CHAPTER TWO

MR WHITMORE, Gemma was told, was in room twenty-three, and no, he had no one with him at that time.

The Ridge Motel was the newest in Lightning Ridge, an ochre-coloured assortment of buildings, with reception and a restaurant separate from the forty units which stood at rectangular attention behind a kidney-shaped pool. Room twenty-three was on the second of the two storeys.

Gemma's stomach was churning as she climbed the stairs, something that would have surprised many people, including Ma, who had often commented on how confident she was for a girl of her upbringing and background. Gemma knew better, recognising her supposed assurance as little more than a desperate weapon to combat her father's volatile and often violent nature. She'd found over the years that if she were *too* docile and subservient he treated her even worse. So she'd learnt to stand up for herself to a degree, sometimes to her sorrow.

But none of that meant she had the sort of *savoir-faire* to deal confidently with a city opal trader like Byron Whitmore. Lord, she was shaking in her boots, or she would have been if she'd been wearing boots! Gemma's only consolation was that she'd decided not to try to sell the big opal today, only the smaller ones.

A couple of nights' sensible thinking since her astonishing find had formulated a plan to take the prize to Sydney and have it valued by a couple of experts before she sold it. It had come to her as late as half an hour ago that it might bring more money if she put it up for auction as a collector's piece. Six-figure amounts kept dancing around in her mind. She'd be able to buy herself a house, pretty clothes, a dog...

Her heart contracted fiercely. No, she wouldn't buy another dog. Not yet. Maybe some day, but not yet. The pain of Blue's death was still too raw, too fresh.

Gemma dragged her mind back to the problems at hand. Selling these infernal opals. By this time she was standing in front of room twenty-three but she couldn't bring herself to knock, gnawing away at her bottom lip instead and trying to find a good reason to abandon this idea entirely.

But that wouldn't get her any money, would it? She'd already booked tickets for the bus leaving tomorrow night for Dubbo, and the train from there to Sydney.

If only her father had let her go with him when he'd sold opals, she groaned silently. If only she'd met this Mr Whitmore before. Ma said he was OK but it was hard totally to dismiss her father's warnings about him.

Oh, get on with it, you stupid girl! Gemma berated herself. God knows how you're going to cope in the big bad city if you can't even do this small thing. Stop being such a wimp!

Taking a deep steadying breath, Gemma curled her fingers into a tight fist and knocked on the door.

'Oh!' she exclaimed when it was wrenched open, practically from under her knuckles. 'Oh!' she cried again, once she'd fully taken in the man who'd opened it.

He was nowhere near fifty, neither did he have black hair or blue eyes. At most he was thirty-five. His hair was a golden wheat colour and his eyes were grey. He was, however, very handsome in an unnervingly sleek, citified sort of way.

'I...I'm sorry, I must have the wrong room,' she babbled. 'I was wanting Mr Whitmore.'

Lazy grey eyes swept down her body and down her long bare tanned legs, one eyebrow arching by the time his gaze lifted back to her face. Gemma stiffened, not sure if his scrutiny was flattering or insulting.

Surely he couldn't be surprised by how she was dressed. No one wore anything other than shorts in Lightning Ridge in the summer, no one except visitors like this chap. *He* was all togged up in tailored grey trousers and a long-sleeved white shirt. There was even a dark red tie at his throat. A travelling salesman, Gemma decided. On his first trip outback, probably. It wouldn't be long before that tie was disposed of and those shirt-sleeves rolled up.

A small smile tugged at his mouth, as though he were amused at something. 'Now I know why Byron always looked forward to his trips out here,' he said drily.

Gemma frowned. Byron? That was Mr Whitmore's first name, wasn't it?

'I'm *Nathan* Whitmore,' the man elaborated before she could put her confusion into words. 'I'm standing in for Byron this trip, a fact that seems to have gotten around. You're my first client this afternoon, and only my third for the day. You *are* a client, aren't you?' he asked, amusement still in his voice.

Gemma was unsure now what to do. Ma had recommended *Byron* Whitmore, not his brother.

'You look concerned, Miss—er...'

'Smith,' she informed him. 'Gemma Smith.'

'Aah... and have you had dealings with my father before, Miss Smith?'

'No, I... your *father*?' Rounded eyes stared into Nathan Whitmore's face, seeing the age lines around his eyes and mouth. Either Byron Whitmore was older than Ma thought or his son had been living the life of a rake. Handsome he might be, but *that* young he wasn't. 'I...I thought you were his brother.'

'I understand your confusion. Byron adopted me when I was seventeen and he was thirty-two. We *are* more like brothers than like father and son.'

'Oh... oh, I see.' She didn't actually. Seventeen was rather old to be adopted. Still, it wasn't any of her business. Her business was getting a good price for the opals in her pocket.

'Let me assure you, Miss Smith,' Nathan Whitmore said, 'that I know opals, and I won't cheat you. Byron would have my hide if I did anything to ruin his reputation for honesty and fairness.'

'He certainly comes highly recommended.'

'Whitmore Opals has a reputation second to none. Shall we go inside, then, and get down to business?'

Gemma hesitated, her eyes darting over Nathan Whitmore's shoulder and into the motel room. It was an oddly personal place to do business in. Intimate, even. Now her eyes darted back to that cool grey gaze.

'Dear Miss Smith,' he said in a rather droll tone, 'I have not come this far to compromise young women, however beautiful they might be.'

Beautiful? He found her *beautiful*?

My God, I'm blushing, she realised, feeling the heat in her face.

Hoping it wouldn't show underneath her tan, she kept her chin up and her eyes steady. He was probably only flattering her, she decided. Hoping, perhaps, to compliment his way into giving her less money than her opals were worth. Ma had warned her about city businessmen. Cunning, ruthless devils, she'd called them only this morning.

But this one didn't look like a devil. More like an angel with that golden hair and that lovely full-lipped mouth.

'Shall we sit down at the table?' he suggested, stepping back to wave her inside.

One swift, all-encompassing glance took in a typical motel room with a king-sized bed in one corner, a built-in television opposite, an extra divan and a round table and two chairs, over the back of which was draped a grey suit jacket.

Gemma chose the other chair and sat down, feeling conscious of her bare legs now, especially since the room was air-conditioned and much cooler than outside. She could appreciate now why its occupant was over-dressed. She clasped her hands together between her knees and gave a little shiver. Even her neck felt cool. If she could have taken her hair down out of its pony-tail she would have.

'The air-conditioning too cold for you? Shall I turn it down?'

'If you would, please, Mr Whitmore.'

How attentive he was, she thought. And how observant. Ma was right. City men were clever. Gemma determined to be on her guard.

The air-conditioning unit hissed when he turned it right off.

'Please call me Nathan,' he said suavely as he sat down, a lock of blond hair falling across his forehead. He swept it aside and smiled at her. 'And may I call you Gemma?'

Despite her earlier resolve not to be distracted by flattery or false charm, Gemma found herself smiling fatuously back at the man opposite her. She nodded, her tongue seemingly thick in her mouth. A light tangy pine smell was wafting across the table from him which she found both pleasant and perturbing. Did all city men smell like that?

'Well, Gemma?' he interrupted her agitated daydreaming. 'I presume you have some opals with you?'

'Oh... oh, yes.' Squirming both physically and mentally, she pulled the small canvas pouch out of her shorts pocket. Fumbling because her fingers were shaking, she finally undid the drawstring and poured the stones out on to the table, then watched with heart pounding while Mr Whitmore put a jeweller's glass to his eye and started examining them.

'Mmm,' he said once. 'Yes, very nice,' another time.

Finally, he put the glass down and looked over at her with a slight frown. 'Did you mine these yourself?'

'No, my father did.'

'And you have his permission to sell them?'

'He died a few days ago,' she said, so bluntly that the man opposite her blinked with astonishment.

'I'm sorry,' he murmured politely.

Then you'd be the only one, Gemma thought.

'You couldn't have known,' she returned, her voice flat.

It brought another sharp glance. 'Do you want individual prices, or are you selling these as a parcel?'

'Which will get me more money?'

He smiled. Gemma noticed that when he smiled he showed lovely white teeth, and a dimple in his right cheek. That was because his smile was slightly lopsided. There was no doubt that he was by far the most attractive man she had ever met, despite his age.

'There are twenty-seven stones here,' he resumed, 'most worth no more than ten dollars. But this one I particularly like.' He pointed to the largest. 'It has a vivid green colour that appeals to me personally. So I'll offer you two hundred and sixty dollars for the rest and one hundred dollars for this one. That's three hundred and sixty in all.'

Gemma remembered what Ma had said about not accepting the first price. 'Four hundred,' she countered with surprising firmness.

He leant back in his chair, breathing in and out quite deeply. Gemma was fascinated by the play of muscles beneath his shirt and his surprisingly broad shoulders. He would look something with that jacket on. 'I was already being over-generous with the three hundred and sixty,' he said.

'Why?'

Gemma's forthright question seemed to startle him for a moment. Then he smiled. 'Well you might ask. Very well. Four hundred. Do you want cash or cheque?'

'Cash.'

'Somehow I knew you were going to say that.'

Extracting a well-stuffed wallet from the breast pocket of the jacket beside him, he counted out four one-hundred-dollar notes before returning the wallet.

They rose simultaneously, Gemma folding the notes and placing them carefully into her back pocket.

'Thank you, Mr Whitmore,' she said, and extended her hand.

He shook it, saying, 'I thought we agreed on Nathan.'

'Sorry,' she grinned. 'I find it hard to call my elders by their first name.' Now that the business end of proceedings was over and Gemma had her money safely tucked away, she was feeling more relaxed.

'Elders,' he repeated, a grimace twisting his mouth. 'Now that's putting me in my place. Might I ask how old you are?'

'Eigh—' Gemma broke off. She'd been going to say eighteen, but of course she wasn't. 'I'll be twenty next month,' she guessed.

He looked surprised, and, for a moment, stared at her hard. She gained the impression he was about to say something but changed his mind, shaking his head instead and walking over to open the door for her.

She walked past him out on to the balcony, but as she went to turn to say thank you one last time, she saw something out of the corner of her eye that made her heart leap and her stomach flip over. For there *he* was, standing down by the pool, looking huge and menacing, watching and waiting for her.

Panic-stricken, she bolted back into the room, almost sending Nathan Whitmore flying. 'Close the door,' she said in a husky, frightened whisper.

'*What*?'

'Close the door!' she hissed, backing up till her knees were against the bed.

He did as she asked, then turned slowly to view her fear-filled face with concern in his. 'What is it? What's out there that's frightened you so much? Is it a man?' he asked sharply. 'Is that it?'

'Yes,' she squeaked, appalled with herself that she'd started to shake uncontrollably. Dear God, she'd always thought herself a brave person. But she wasn't brave at all. Not even a little bit.

'Your boyfriend?'

She shook her head vigorously.

'Who, then? Dear God, what did he do to you to make you react like this?'

He was standing in front of her now, holding her trembling shoulders with firm but gentle hands.

Memories of other male hands surfaced from the backwater of her mind, large calloused hands that pinched and poked and probed...

A strangled sob broke from her lips, haunted eyes flying to warm grey ones.

'It's all right,' the owner of those eyes soothed. 'You're safe here with me.'

Another sob welled up within her and all of a sudden, she was wrapping her arms around him and hugging him for dear life, a whole torrent of emotions cascading through her, leaving her awash with a fiercely instinctive need to hold and be held.

After a momentary hesitation, Nathan Whitmore answered that need, holding her tightly against him, stroking her neck and back with fatherly tenderness, whispering soothing words as one would to a frightened child. But there was nothing fatherly in the effect such an intensely intimate embrace eventually had on his male body, nothing fatherly at all.

Nathan abruptly held her away from him, pressing her down into a sitting position on the bed. 'I'll get you a drink,' he said curtly, and turned away before the situation became embarrassing. 'And then you're going to tell me what the problem is,' he called back over his shoulder.

Gemma stared after him as he crossed the room, her head whirling with an alien confusion. Who would have thought she would ever find a safe haven in the solid warmth of a man's chest, or enjoy the feel of male arms encircling her?

She was still looking up at Nathan with startled surprise when he returned with a glass of brandy. For a moment their eyes locked and she could have sworn his were as puzzled as her own.

'Here.' He pressed the glass into her hands. 'Drink this up. Then start talking.'

In a way it was a relief to tell someone after keeping it to herself all these years. But she'd been so ashamed at the time. She'd felt so dirty. Yet the words did not come easily. She stumbled over them, faltering occasionally, and finding it hard to explain exactly what had happened.

'So he didn't actually rape you,' Nathan said with relief in his voice after listening to her tortured tale.

'He...he tried,' she explained huskily, 'but he...he...couldn't d-do it. He was very drunk.'

'And where were your parents while this was happening?'

'My mother's dead,' she explained. 'My father had passed out. He'd been drinking. *He* came home with him. When Dad fell asleep he climbed into my bed. When I screamed, he put one hand over my mouth while he...he...you know what he did,' she finished in a raw whisper.

'And does this bastard have a name?'

Gemma shuddered and shook her head. 'I never found out and I never asked. I...I see him in town sometimes, watching me.'

'But he hasn't come near you since.'

'No, but now that my father's dead, I...I'm scared.'

'How did your father die?'

'He fell down a mine shaft.'

'Are you sure he fell?'

Gemma blinked her astonishment.

'I think we should go to the police and tell them about this creep,' Nathan decided.

Gemma gasped and jumped to her feet. 'No! I don't want to do that. I can't tell them what I've just told you. I simply can't! Besides, I...I'm leaving Lightning Ridge tomorrow, on the bus.'

'To go where?'

'To Sydney.'

He stared at her for a long moment. 'Sydney's a tough town for someone alone,' he said. 'Do you have any relatives there?'

'I'm not sure.'

'Don't you *know*?'

She shrugged. 'My mother was born in Sydney but I never knew her folks. I . . . I was hoping I might be able to track them down some time.'

'How much money do you have?'

'Enough.'

His smile was sardonic. 'Independent, aren't you? Look, I'll give you my card. If you find yourself in a hole when you get to Sydney, or you're desperate for a job, look me up, OK?' Striding back over to his suit jacket, he drew a small white card from another of the pockets and brought it back to her.

'Tell me what I can do to help right now,' he added after she'd slipped the card into the breast pocket of her blue checked shirt. 'Did you drive yourself here? Can I walk you to your car?'

'Yes, I'd appreciate that.'

'And what about when you get home?'

'That'll be all right. Ma will be there.'

Nathan frowned at her. 'But I thought you said your mother was dead.'

'She is. Ma's not my mother. She's a friend.'

He sighed. 'Something tells me you're a very complicated girl.'

Gemma laughed. 'Ma says I have hidden qualities. Is that the same thing as complicated?'

'Could very well be. But I don't think I should try to find out.' Having uttered this rather cryptic remark, he picked up his room key, took Gemma's elbow and ushered her outside. 'Can you still see him?' he asked.

Gemma's heart pounded as she looked around. 'No,' she sighed.

'Right, well, let's get you safely home.'

CHAPTER THREE

'SHE'S become impossible, Nathan. Simply impossible!' Lenore glared at her ex-husband as he sat behind that damned desk of his, looking not the slightest bit perturbed.

'Kirsty is a typical teenager. You shouldn't let her upset you so.'

'That's easy for you to say. You don't have to live with her.' Lenore slumped down into a chair and sighed heavily. 'I'm at my wits' end. They're threatening to expel her from school. She's smoking on the sly, swears like a trooper and dresses like a trollop. I...I've been thinking of sending her to boarding-school,' she finished, flicking a nervous glance at Nathan through her long lashes.

Lenore knew what he thought of boarding-school, having been dumped into different ones by his drug-crazed mother whenever a new man came on to the scene, only to be dragged out once she was alone again and wanting company. By the time he was sixteen a totally screwed-up Nathan had run away from the latest five-star school, just in time to find his mother, dead from a heroin overdose.

With such a history, it was no wonder Lenore felt a little edgy about suggesting boarding-school for their daughter.

Nathan reacted just as she'd feared.

'She won't be going to bloody boarding-school,' he bit out, snapping forward on his chair. 'She can come live with me for a while.'

Lenore's lovely green eyes widened with genuine surprise, then narrowed into a frown. 'Where? Not at that beach-house of yours. Who would mind her till you got home from work?'

'I'm living at Belleview till Byron gets out of hospital and on his feet again.'

'Oh, yes, I forgot. Poor Byron. How's his leg?'

'On the mend. He might have to use a cane for a while, though.'

'He'll hate that.'

'Better than being dead, like Irene. Though maybe Irene's death isn't such a tragedy. She was a miserable bitch, and she made Byron miserable too.'

'For heaven's sake, Nathan, don't you ever have any pity for anyone?' Lenore snapped, irritated with this hard man whom she'd tried to love, but failed. He just wouldn't meet her halfway. Or even a quarter way.

'I have pity for a daughter whose mother doesn't want her around,' he said coldly.

'That's not true and you know it! Oh, Nathan, you can be so cruel sometimes. Cruel and heartless.' Tears flooded her eyes and she rummaged in her handbag for a tissue.

Nathan watched her mop up her tears without turning a hair.

'Let's get back to the point, shall we?' he said when she was sufficiently composed. 'I suggest you go home, get Kirsty to pack her things and bring her round tonight after dinner. But if she comes to live with me, she comes for a whole term at least. No chopping and changing midstream.'

Lenore felt as though a huge weight had been lifted from her shoulders. Maybe Nathan would straighten the girl out a bit. Kirsty loved her father. And Nathan loved her too. His daughter was the only female who'd ever been able to get past the steely cover Nathan kept around his heart.

Kirsty was the main reason Nathan had married Lenore. That, and his mistaken belief that she would be the sort of wife to suit him: an independent woman who wouldn't lean or demand, who would be there at his side when he needed a social partner, and there, in his bed, when he needed sex.

Well, Lenore had needed more than that. Much more. So after twelve years of the loneliest marriage she could ever imagine she'd called it quits. People had condemned her for their divorce, saying she'd put her acting career in front of her husband. And maybe there was a bit of truth in that. But she had to have *something*.

A depressing sigh wafted from Lenore's lips. If only things had been different with Zachary all those years ago. If only he hadn't been married. If only he'd loved her as intensely as she'd loved him, as she still loved him.

'If you've finished daydreaming...' Nathan drawled caustically.

Lenore blinked and looked up.

'Maybe you'd like to tell me what or who is bringing that wistful look into your eyes. Surely not Kirsty. It wouldn't be Zachary Marsden, would it?'

'And if it is?' she retorted, piqued by his sarcasm. 'Don't tell me you're jealous, Nathan. Jealousy is an emotion reserved for people in love. You never loved me any more than I loved you so don't pretend now, thank you very much.'

'I never pretended a thing with you, Lenore. It was you who seduced me in the first place, you who used *my* body, not the other way around, you who pretended I meant more to you than I ever could mean.'

'Are you saying you *wanted* me to be in love with you?' she asked, disbelieving.

'I'm saying no man likes to be had on the rebound. We could have had a good marriage, if it hadn't been for Zachary Marsden lurking around in your heart. We could still have had a good marriage if you hadn't indulged in sentimental rubbish and deliberately kept your supposed love for him alive. Do you think I didn't notice how often you contrived to put yourself in Zachary's company? The poor bastard. You've done nothing but tease

him for years. You know he's a decent sort of man, that
he wants to stay faithful to his wife and family. Give him
a break and find someone else to try out your *femme fa-
tale* talents on.'

'Oh!' Lenore jumped to her feet. 'Oh, you're just impossible! You don't understand true love. But one day,
Nathan, one day you're going to really fall in love and
then you'll know what it's like. Who knows? Maybe it'll
make you human, like the rest of us. Maybe I might even
learn to like you, as I once mistakenly thought I did.'

Gemma was sitting in a deep leather two-seater in the
plush reception area of Whitmore Opals when the most
stunning-looking woman she'd ever seen stormed out of
Nathan's office, masses of gorgeous red hair flying out
behind a face so arrestingly beautiful that one could only
stare. She banged the door shut behind her before covering her luminescent green eyes with sunglasses and
striding across the grey-blue carpet on the way towards
the exit.

''Bye, Moira,' she threw at the receptionist on her way
past. 'My commiserations that you have to work for that
man. He's impossible!'

'Goodbye, Mrs Whitmore,' the middle-aged receptionist called after her.

Gemma's head snapped round to stare after the red-
head. So! Nathan Whitmore was married.

She shook her head, smiling ruefully at her own stu-
pidity. Of course a man like him would be married.

Gemma almost laughed at the silly thoughts that had
been tumbling through her head since she'd parted company with Nathan in Lightning Ridge three days before.
It had been crazy of her to imagine he'd been genuinely
attracted to her, that he'd been loath to let her go. He'd
simply been kind to her, that was all. Nothing more.

I'm as naïve as Ma said, Gemma realised with some
dismay.

When she'd told Ma about what happened at the motel, the old woman had been aghast.

'Good God, girl, and there I was thinkin' you'd got your head screwed on where men were concerned. But you're just as silly as the rest. Fancy huggin' a stranger like that in his motel room. And acceptin' a drink as well. The danger wasn't from that ugly old bugger outside, love, but the handsome one inside!'

Gemma didn't agree with Ma about that. She was sure Nathan Whitmore was a good man. But she had to agree about herself. Clearly, she was as vulnerable to a handsome face as the next girl, and twice as silly as most. Her actions in that motel room had been incredibly naïve and foolish. If Nathan hadn't been an honourable man, God knew what might have happened, for there was no doubting she'd been blown away by how she'd felt when in his arms. Her only consolation was that the incident had eliminated her worry that a man's touch would repel her.

The receptionist stood up from behind her desk and went over to knock on the door that Mrs Whitmore had slammed shut. After a brusque command to enter, she went inside, exiting a few seconds later with a polite smile on her face. 'Mr Whitmore will see you straight away, Miss Smith. Please go right in.'

Gemma stood up, feeling suddenly fat and frumpish in her new pink cotton sundress with its tight bodice constraining her full breasts. Yet that morning, she had thought she looked...inviting. But seeing Nathan's wife, so sophisticated and slim in a green silk suit, had put a dent in Gemma's confidence over her appearance. She should have left her hair out, she thought unhappily, not tied it up into a childish pony-tail with an even more childish pink ribbon.

A dampening dismay was beginning to invade when Gemma checked her self-pity with a stern hand. What did it matter what she looked like? The man was married. Decent girls did not try to attract married men. And she was a decent girl. Or so she hoped.

Clutching the straw handbag in which she'd placed her precious legacy that morning, Gemma lifted her chin and strode purposefully into the office. But the moment her gaze rested once more on that handsome blond head and those fascinating grey eyes, she was lost.

Was she imagining things or was he looking at her the way some of the male customers at the café back at the Ridge had started looking at her? As though they'd like to have *her* on their plate and not a hamburger and chips. Gemma was quietly appalled that for the first time in her life she liked being looked at like that.

His hunger was fleeting, however, if that was what she'd glimpsed, Nathan Whitmore getting to his feet and coming round to shake her hand with a cool and impersonal politeness. 'Miss Smith,' he said matter-of-factly. 'How nice to see you again. Would you like to sit down while I get the door?' And he indicated an upright wooden-backed chair that sat in front of the desk.

Gemma sat down, trying not to look as depressed as she suddenly felt. Couldn't he at least have called her Gemma?

She watched him walk back round behind his impressive desk, equally impressive in a dark blue suit which fitted his body to perfection and highlighted his golden hair. He'd had it cut since she last saw him, she realised, for when he bent forward slightly on sitting down no wayward lock fell in boyish disarray across his forehead. The sleek, ultra-groomed look gave him a crisp, no-nonsense, almost forbidding air which she still found disturbingly attractive.

Her mind flew to his wife and her dramatic exit. What had he said or done to upset her so much? Why had she called him impossible?

The man who'd been so kind to her out at the Ridge was far from impossible. He'd been sweet. Sweet and warm and caring. Still, it appeared that man had been left behind in the outback of Australia. The pragmatic individual sitting behind his city desk in his plush city office seemed like a different person.

'So, how can I help you?' he opened up.

Gemma stared at him. No questions about how she was, or how was her trip to Sydney, or where was she staying, just straight down to brass tacks. Her disappointment was sharp, but she gathered herself to answer coolly.

'I have an opal I would like valued.' If he was going to be all business, then so was she. 'You do valuations here, don't you?'

'We do.'

'I realise they aren't free. I'm quite prepared to pay whatever the going price is.'

He waived her offer with a dismissive gesture of his hand. 'That won't be necessary. Do you have this opal with you?'

'Yes.'

'I could give you a reasonable estimate immediately, if you like.' He smiled, and she felt a lurch in her stomach.

'Thank you. I'd appreciate that.' Gemma was only too glad to drag her eyes away from that handsome smiling face to dig the opal out from the depths of her handbag. She'd wrapped it in an old checked teatowel. As she stood up to place her treasure on the desk before him, butterflies crowded her stomach. What if it wasn't worth as much as she hoped? What if she'd been mistaken about its rarity? Maybe it would prove to be flawed in some way. She didn't have any experience with opals of this size and quality. Nathan leant over and picked the stone up, turning it over in his hands as she had done.

'My God,' was the first thing he said, his voice a shocked whisper.

He peered down at the black opal for a long time, turning it this way and that to catch the brilliant and glowing flashes of light. Finally, his gaze snapped up to hers. 'Where did you get this?' he demanded to know.

Gemma was startled by the accusation in his question. It flustered her. 'I... I... my father left it to me.'

'And where did *he* get it?'

She blinked. 'I suppose he found it. In one of his claims.'

'I doubt that very much,' he said slowly.

Gemma's mind was racing. What was he thinking? That Dad *stole* it?

This solution to her father's possessing such a treasure had not occurred to Gemma before. The ramifications of it being true struck a severe blow. Ashen-faced, she stared across at the man peering at her with steely eyes.

'You think he stole it, don't you?' she cried.

When Nathan didn't deny it, she groaned, and slumped back into her chair.

'Oh, my God...' Her head dropped into her hands, all her dreams crumbling on the spot. She should have known, should have guessed. Her father would have sold that opal if he'd had a legal right to it. But he hadn't... And neither did she...

'Gemma...'

She glanced up through soggy lashes to see Nathan squatting beside her chair. His face had softened to a semblance of the face she remembered from the motel and her heart turned over.

'I have no proof at this moment that your opal was stolen,' he said gently, 'but it resembles a stone that disappeared over twenty years ago. If you like, I can have it looked at by the man who owned it before it vanished. Believe me when I say you will not get into trouble, no matter what happens.'

'Who... who is the rightful owner?'

'If it is the opal I think it is, then it's Byron... my father.'

Gemma gasped. 'But how incredible!'

'Not so incredible. There was a time when Whitmore Opals was one of the only two opal-trading companies in New South Wales. They owned many precious opals, this one included.'

A thought struck Gemma and she frowned. 'How do I know you're telling me the truth?'

Nathan stood up, his eyes cooling. 'The theft was registered with the police at the time, as was a detailed description of the opal. You can check it out if you like.'

Gemma felt small for having doubted him. 'No,' she mumbled. 'I believe you.'

'If you like I will have a photograph taken of the opal and give you a receipt for it, then if it turns out not to be the opal in question it will be returned to you. Of course, if this happens, we would like the opportunity to buy it from you. An opal of this beauty and rarity does not come up for sale very often.'

Gemma decided it would be foolish to be too trusting, so she accepted this offer, at the same time agreeing to give Whitmore Opals first right of purchase. But intuition told her this would never come about. The opal had not legally been her father's, and it would never legally be hers. All her dreams had been dashed. Suddenly, she was here in Sydney, staying in a cheap hotel, with just under a thousand dollars in her purse, no job, no friends and no opal.

A deep depression settled on her, making her shoulders sag.

'I'll have Moira get you a cup of coffee while you wait,' Nathan said. 'Or would you prefer tea?'

'No, coffee,' she said limply.

'Black or white?'

'White with one sugar.'

Moira brought her a couple of biscuits with the coffee, which Gemma ate gratefully, knowing she would have to conserve her money now. She was thinking about what her next move would be when Nathan returned with the photo and receipt, and a black leather briefcase.

'I'll take the opal to the hospital for Byron to look at this afternoon,' he said, patting the briefcase.

'The hospital?'

'Byron was in a boating accident a few weeks back. He was lucky to survive. His wife and a couple of friends were killed.'

'Oh, how awful! The poor man.'

'Yes.'

Gemma interpreted Nathan's curt tone as grief, since Byron's wife would have been his adopted mother. But his closed face didn't allow gushes of sympathy and she fell silent.

'I can understand this opal business has come as a great shock to you,' Nathan resumed. 'You were probably relying on the money. But I'm sure Byron will give you a substantial monetary reward for its return.'

Gemma brightened. 'Do you think so?'

'I guarantee it. Call back in the morning and I'll have either the reward for you, or your opal back again. Where are you staying, by the way?'

'The Central Hotel for the present.'

A dark frown scrunched up his high forehead.

'That's no place for a young girl like you to be staying. Look, you'd better come home with me. We've plenty of rooms, then tomorrow we'll see if we can't find you a decent flat.' He glanced at his watch. 'Come on, I'll take you to your hotel right now and get your things, then I'll drive you home to Belleview.'

Gemma scrambled to her feet. 'Oh, but I . . . I can't let you do that. What will your wife say?'

'My wife?'

'Yes. Mrs Whitmore.'

His smile was ironic. 'I dare say Mrs Whitmore might have plenty to say. But it won't make a blind bit of difference. Lenore Langtry ceased to be my legal spouse two years ago. Does that put your sweet mind at rest?'

No, Gemma thought as he swept her out of his office. Not at all, she reaffirmed once she found herself being settled into the most luxurious car she'd ever seen. Most definitely not, when Nathan stayed leaning over her for a second longer than necessary, peering down her cleavage then up into her eyes with an expression no female could mistake a second time.

Ma's warnings came back to haunt her. What was she getting herself into here? This was no schoolboy she was going home with. They were *easy* to ward off. Neither was he a safely married man with a chaperoning wife in tow. He was a mature man, a divorced man, a ... a *city* man. And she was letting him take her home for the night. Ma would be having apoplexy by now if she knew!

But no sooner were they under way than Nathan started chatting away with her quite naturally, putting her at ease, making her feel very relaxed in his company. Soon she began wondering if Ma's warnings had made her paranoid about city men. So he'd glanced at her a couple of times. What did she expect after wearing this type of bare-necked dress? She'd bought it specifically with Nathan Whitmore in mind after all. Oh, she'd denied it to Ma at the time, but there was no point in denying it to herself. She'd wanted him to look at her and he had. But looking was only looking. Nothing to work up a head of steam about.

Finally, the questions came about her trip down and her impressions of Sydney, Nathan listening with gentlemanly politeness as she babbled on about how large and intimidating she found everything, how she hadn't been able to sleep the night before because of the traffic noise, how she thought everything was awfully expensive, even a rather dingy hotel room.

'I don't think I'll ever get used to a sandwich costing over three dollars,' she said, with awe in her voice.

'Yes, you will,' he returned drily, then smiled across at her. 'But not too soon, I hope. I like you just the way you are.'

Gemma flushed with pleasure at what she saw as his seal of approval. He liked her. He really liked her. How exciting. Not even thinking about Ma or her warnings could still her dancing heart.

It must have taken them over an hour to get from the city office block which housed Whitmore Opals down to the hotel then back over the Harbour Bridge. But Gemma didn't really mind. Her eyes were everywhere. There was no doubt that, despite the claustrophobic feeling the city gave her, it had the most beautiful setting in the world.

Her mouth remained open as they drove across the Bridge. There was so much to see with Darling Harbour and the Opera House and the Quay and all that lovely blue water. How different from the dry, dusty, grey crater-filled landscape that had been her world for eighteen years.

No, twenty, she corrected herself again, a frown forming as she remembered her other mission in coming to Sydney. Would she be able to find out more about her mother? A trip to the registry of Births, Deaths and Marriages would be a start. Hopefully, she'd be able to get a copy of her parents' marriage certificate, which she hadn't located among her father's things. Then there were electoral rolls to check. Motor registry lists, maybe. Driving licences, perhaps.

But would the authorities give her such information freely? If not, maybe the missing-persons division of the police could help, because she certainly couldn't afford a private detective. Not now. She had to be very careful with her money. And she simply had to get a job.

'Mr Whitmore. Nathan...'

'Mmm?'

'Do...do you think there might be a job for me at Whitmore Opals? I've learnt a lot about opals over the years, you know.'

'I'm sure you have. What would you like to do?'

'I don't know. I could serve behind the counter, I guess. Do you have shops like that, ones that sell opals to the public? Or do you just make jewellery?'

'We have two retail outlets. One down at the Rocks, and one in the foyer of Regency Hotel. Yes, I'm sure we could use someone with your knowledge behind the counter, though you'd be required to do a course in Japanese first. A lot of our customers are Japanese businessmen and tourists.'

'How long would it take me to learn Japanese?' she asked, concerned about her money situation, not to mention her ability to learn another language. She'd only been average at school.

'With intensive lessons, most people are able to communicate on a basic level after a couple of months.'

'A couple of months! But I'll have run out of money by then.'

'I doubt that. I'm sure Byron will be very generous with his reward. That opal is conservatively worth over a million dollars.'

'You're joking!' Gemma gasped.

'Not at all. Prices are on the rise again.'

'A million dollars . . .'

'Are you upset that you're probably not going to be an instant millionaire?'

'Yes,' she admitted. 'I am.'

'Money doesn't always make you happy, Gemma.'

She laughed. 'Neither does being poor.'

Now *he* laughed. 'You could be right there. Well, at least you have a better chance than most poor people of ending up rich.'

'How do you figure that out?'

His head turned to rake over her once more. And once again, Gemma was shocked. Not so much by what she saw behind those grey eyes, but by the way they could make her feel. All hot and heady and helpless.

'A beautiful young girl like yourself should have no trouble ensnaring a rich husband. Who knows? I might even marry you myself.'

Gemma sat there, stunned. Till he bestowed a wry little smile on her and she realised he was only teasing.

'You shouldn't make fun of me,' she said with reproach in her voice, but turmoil in her heart. For she would marry him in a flash if he asked her, this man she'd only met twice, but who already had her in the palm of his hand. It was a shocking realisation and one which underlined her own foolishness where Nathan Whitmore was concerned.

Gemma had often wondered why women made fools of themselves over men, not having ever understood the strange power of that alien emotion, love. She'd also scorned girls who claimed to have fallen in love at first sight. What rubbish! she had used to think.

Now, as she wallowed beneath the onslaught of a tidal force of longing, she had to accept she'd been wrong. This had to be love, this dreadful drowning feeling, this mad desire to go along with anything and everything this man suggested, even something as insane as marrying him.

But of course he hadn't meant it. She had to keep reminding herself of that. No doubt city men couldn't resist teasing silly, naïve country girls. She simply had to pull herself together.

He was smiling at her again, amusement in his eyes. 'Who says I was making fun of you?'

A very real resentment began to simmer inside Gemma, who was not a person to simmer in silence. 'I can just see you marrying someone like me,' she countered indignantly. 'People would think you'd gone mad after having someone like Mrs Whitmore as your wife. Now *she's* what I call beautiful!'

'Is she now?' he drawled. 'Yes, well, Lenore is lovely to look at, no one would deny. But there are all kinds of beauty, my dear Gemma, and all kinds of wives. Speaking of which, you'll be meeting Lenore tonight. She's bringing my daughter over to stay for a while. Apparently, the little minx has been creating merry hell at home and is in need of a firm hand.'

'How old is she?' Gemma asked, picturing a recalcitrant six-year-old.

'Fourteen.'

Her head snapped round before she could stop it.

'Yes, I know,' he said drily. 'I was a child groom. Twenty-one years young the day before my wedding. And yes, it was a shotgun affair.'

Gemma caught his bitter tone and wondered if his marriage had been under duress right from the start. Marriage simply because the woman was pregnant seemed fraught with danger. The couple had to be in love as well. Still, it was hard to imagine a man not being in love with Lenore Whitmore. Maybe Nathan's bitterness came from her not being in love with him.

'Kirsty's basically a good kid,' Nathan went on. 'But the divorce hit her hard. She just can't seem to come to terms with it. Not that I blame her.'

'You . . . you shouldn't be bothering with me, then, if you've got your daughter coming.'

'Why not? As I said, there's plenty of room. Besides, you're not that much older than Kirsty. She might relate to you better than Melanie or Ava.'

'Melanie and Ava?' Gemma must have sounded as perplexed as she felt, for Nathan chuckled.

'Don't worry. I haven't got a harem installed. Melanie's Byron's housekeeper. She's not that old—thirtyish, I guess—but unfortunately projects a personality that would make Mrs Danvers seem warm.'

'Who's Mrs Danvers? The previous housekeeper?'

Nathan smiled. 'A housekeeper certainly, but one of the fictional kind. I'll tell you about her one day.'

'Perhaps you should tell me who Ava is first.'

'Ah, Ava. She's Byron's kid sister. A change-of-life baby. As scatty as anything and young at heart, but as old as Melanie. No, I think Kirsty'll get along best with you. In fact, I might hire you as her minder while you learn Japanese. What do you say? Bed and board for nix in exchange for keeping an eye on the little devil before and after school?'

Gemma's head was whirling. Everything seemed to be going so fast. In the beginning, she'd only been going to stay the night. 'I . . . I'll have to think about it.'

'Will you? Pity. I was hoping you'd just say yes. It would have been the perfect solution.' His sideways glance carried an odd little smile which Gemma found quite unnerving. It was as though it hid some secret plan only he was privy to.

'P-perfect solution?' she found herself stammering.

'Yes. *You* would be safely accommodated till you find your feet and *I* wouldn't have to worry about my wayward daughter. Still, I have to warn you, Gemma, I don't take no for an answer lightly. I can be a very stubborn man when I want something.'

Gemma gulped. She didn't doubt him for a moment. But what, exactly, was he wanting?

Oh, Ma...I'm trying to keep my head. I really am. But it's hard. It's really hard. If only he weren't so...so...

'How long before we get to your place?' she blurted out, her stomach in knots.

'Not far now. But it's not my home. It's Byron's. It's called Belleview Manor. But mostly we just call it Belleview.'

CHAPTER FOUR

FOR a girl who had spent her entire life living in a dirt-walled dugout, Gemma's introduction to Belleview was an overwhelming experience.

'My God!' she gasped when Nathan swung his dark blue sedan into a driveway, stopping in front of high iron gates which had the name 'Belleview' carved into one of the sandstone gate-posts. They'd been travelling along a quiet, tree-lined avenue for some time, in a suburb called St Ives, where Gemma had already glimpsed some splendid homes behind high security walls, but this...this was something else.

'I agree. It *is* rather ostentatious,' Nathan said, pressing some sort of remote-control unit so that the gates began opening all by themselves.

'Oh, no,' Gemma denied, embarrassed that he might think she was criticising his home. 'It's the most beautiful house I've ever seen. Why, it's even more beautiful than Tara in *Gone With The Wind*. In fact, it looks a bit like Tara.'

'I suppose it does, superficially. All those white columns. But it's a lot more modern inside. More modern than Tara, that is. Certainly not all that modern by today's standard. It was built by Byron's father in 1947, just after the war. Byron has made some renovations over the years, however. Put in air-conditioning and a pool.'

The gates now properly open, the car purred forwards, following the curve of the red gravel driveway to stop in front of the huge two-storey white mansion. Gemma couldn't stop admiring the house and gardens. There was so much colour. And the lawns were so green.

But it was the pond complete with lilies in the centre of
the circular driveway that entranced her the most, perhaps because water had been such a sparse commodity
out at Lightning Ridge.

'This is like something out of a fairy-tale,' she said,
and beamed across at Nathan.

The corner of his mouth lifted in one of those small
sardonic smiles which Gemma wasn't sure she liked any
more. Did he always view the world with that air of wryly
amused cynicism?

'And who are you in this fairy-tale?' he asked. 'Cin-
derella?'

Gemma's face fell with his mocking tone. She turned
away so that he wouldn't see how hurt she was. When she
went to get out of the car, he stopped her with a hand on
her arm.

'I'm sorry, Gemma.'

His gentle apology moved her so much that she almost burst into tears. With great difficulty Gemma controlled herself and turned back to face him. A foolish
move. He was very close, having leant over to grab her
arm; so close that she could smell that pine-scented aftershave he always wore.

She stared into his eyes and a trembling started deep
within. His hand lifted to lay against her cheek. Amazingly, it too was far from steady.

'God, but you're lovely,' he muttered thickly, and,
curling his hand around the back of her neck, he slowly
began to pull her mouth to his.

She gasped back from him, brown eyes wide like those
of a startled fawn. 'No!'

Her rejection clearly shocked him. Or was it himself he
was shocked at? 'I was only going to kiss you, Gemma,'
he said sharply, 'not ravish you. Do you think I would try
to force myself on you like that brute you told me about?'

'No,' she admitted shakily. 'You're nothing like him.
You're nothing like any man I've ever met! But I hardly
know you, after all. And I...I...' Her words trailed into
a dazed silence, her thoughts a mess.

'What you're saying is that you're not that type of girl. Do you think I don't already know that, Gemma? You're the sweetest, nicest girl I've ever met. Do you honestly think I invited you home tonight with the sole intention of having my wicked way with you?'

Her blush was fierce, her embarrassment total. When he actually put it into words she felt a fool.

'If you're having second thoughts,' he said coldly, 'then we can turn round right now and find you a hotel near by.'

'No!' Gemma burst out. The thought that she might have offended Nathan, who'd been so good to her, was unthinkable. 'I'm sorry, Nathan. Truly. I...I know you're a gentleman.'

'I like to think I am, though you do have a way of making me do things on the spur of the moment, like that kiss. You must know how lovely you are, Gemma. Lovely and desirable and very very tempting.'

'T-tempting?'

'Yes, tempting. Damn it all, perhaps I *should* take you to a hotel!'

He might have driven off too, if a white sports car hadn't careered into the driveway at that moment, screaming round to screech to a gravel-scrunching halt right in front of them. The driver's door was flung open and a young woman unfolded herself from behind the wheel, a wild-looking creature with very short, impossibly white hair and kohl-rimmed eyes, which flashed curiosity at Nathan once she spied Gemma in the car beside him.

Gemma stared as the girl strode over, her tall athletic body looking extremely sexy in tight white jeans slung low on her hips and a man's white shirt tied around her tanned midriff. Outlandish gold loops dangled from her ears, and she had to be wearing a dozen gold bracelets, which jingled and jangled as she walked. They weren't the only things that moved as she walked, her generous breasts clearly braless beneath the shirt.

'Hi, there, darls. I'm back,' she said, pouting full pink lips at Nathan through the driver's window.

'So I see,' he returned drily. 'I thought you were mending your grief-stricken heart with Roberto in Fiji.'

'Nah. He turned out to be a drag. No fun at all.'

'You mean he wouldn't jump when you said jump.'

The girl pulled a face at him then cocked her head to one side as she surveyed Gemma, who must have been still staring with her mouth open.

'Who's this, brother, dear? Some stray you picked up off the streets?'

'Watch your mouth, Jade,' Nathan snapped.

'Oooh, you've gone all masterly and protective.' She gave Gemma a more thorough once-over. 'Mmm. Not your usual style, Nathan, dear. And it's bordering on cradle-snatching.'

'Jade,' he warned darkly.

'All right, all right, I'll behave. You do have that effect on me, don't you? So, are you going to introduce us? No, I suppose you aren't. I'm Jade Whitmore, darls....' And, leaning into the car through the window so that one of her breasts was practically stuffed into Nathan's face, she shook Gemma's hand. 'My, you *are* pretty. I'm Nathan's adopted sister, by the way, only daughter of Byron and his dear recently departed wife, Irene.'

'Jade, for God's sake!' Nathan finally lost his temper and shoved her back out through the window. 'Don't take any damned notice of her, Gemma. She has this tasteless sense of humour and no tact at all.'

'Which makes me just the opposite to you, Nathan, dear,' Jade countered airily. 'You have no sense of humour and all the tact in the world. So it's Gemma, is it?'

She bent over, showing ample cleavage as she peered into the car from a safe distance. 'Well, Gemma, watch yourself with this so-called brother of mine. He has the habit of making silly women like us fall madly in love with him, but he doesn't ever love them back. Oh, he'll make love to you. And very well too, for a machine. But when it comes to matters of the heart, you'll find out he just hasn't got one.'

By this time Nathan was getting out of the car, his expression coldly threatening.

'Now don't get mad, Nathan,' Jade laughed, wagging a finger at him. 'I'm going. I've decided even Roberto is better than nothing. And that's all I've ever got from this place. Nothing!'

Gemma glimpsed a flash of the most crushing pain in the girl's face before she whirled away and dashed back into her car. Gravel flying, she accelerated away, leaving a furious-looking Nathan glaring after her.

Heaving a frustrated sigh, he turned to face Gemma, who was sitting in stunned silence in the passenger seat. Nathan walked round and wrenched the door open.

'You might as well get out and come inside. Don't worry. You'll be safe enough now. Jade has a sobering effect on most people, especially me.'

Gemma climbed out, her mind still on the vivid Jade and that shattered look.

'I think she's very unhappy,' she murmured.

'If she is, it's her own damned stupid fault,' Nathan stated. 'She would have to be the most selfish, spoilt, wilful woman I've ever known. No, she's not a woman. She's a child, with a typical child's way of only wanting what she can't have.'

Namely you, Gemma guessed, her thoughts flying back to Jade's astonishing hint that Nathan had once taken her to bed. Had he? she wondered. She didn't dare ask but she rather suspected he might have. Nathan pretended to be a cool, controlled man, but Gemma knew better. Hiding behind that urbane manner lay a man whose hand could tremble when it touched a woman's cheek, and whose voice could grow thick with desire in a split-second. What had Jade said about him?

'He'll make love to you... and very well too, for a machine. But when it comes to matters of the heart, you'll find he just hasn't got one...'

Gemma's mind whirled over those words as she stood on the flagstone patio, waiting while Nathan lifted her old black suitcase from the boot of the car. Jade was wrong about that last part, she decided. Nathan did have a heart. He just didn't like to wear it on his sleeve. But the other part about his making love to *her*... Such a thought sent a shiver rippling down Gemma's spine.

'Don't let anything Jade said worry you,' Nathan advised on joining her. 'She's an incorrigible liar and a troublemaker of the first order. As if *I* would ever make love to someone like her.' He shuddered in revulsion. 'I'm just thankful she decided to leave again. The longer she stays away, the better!'

Lenore bundled a sulky Kirsty into the car straight after dinner, and set out for the relatively short drive from her villa home in Turramurra to Belleview.

'I keep telling you, I don't *want* to go live in that ghastly old mausoleum!' Kirsty complained. 'It's not as though Dad'll ever be there. Not in spirit, anyway. He works at Whitmore Opals all day, writes those boring old plays of his all night, then goes down to the beach-house to write all weekend!'

Lenore resisted arguing with her daughter. Setting her lips firmly, she simply kept on driving.

'Why can't you and Dad get back together again?' Kirsty resumed in a whiny voice. 'He didn't want a divorce. He told me so. It's your fault. You and your stupid bloody career!'

'If you keep using that disgusting language,' Lenore threatened her daughter, 'I'll wash your mouth out with soap.'

'You and whose army?'

'Wait till I tell your father the way you're speaking to me!'

'I'm shaking in my boots.'

Lenore shot a truly pained look across at her daughter, who looked sorry for a second, before she lifted her nose in a disdainful sniff and turned her face away. But not before Lenore saw tears pricking at Kirsty's eyes.

Lenore felt like crying herself. Maybe Kirsty was right. Maybe it *was* all her fault. Did she expect too much from life? Should she have settled for a lonely, loveless marriage? Struggled on regardless?

She hadn't really been happy since the divorce, despite having a lot more success on the stage. Already, she'd secured a marvellous meaty part in a play this year, rehearsals to start next week. As for being lonely…well, she was still lonely. She hadn't been with a man in two years for one thing, yet she enjoyed sex. Nathan had been an expert lover, knowing exactly what buttons to push to turn her on even when she wasn't in the mood. But their lovemaking had never been anything but a meeting of bodies in bed, often in the dark. She could have been any woman and it wouldn't have mattered to Nathan.

But men were like that, weren't they? That was why prostitution was the oldest profession. They could separate love and sex. No trouble.

Maybe some women could too, but in the end Lenore had not been one of them. Slowly but surely, she hadn't been able to stand the way she felt after Nathan rolled from her and invariably fell into a sound sleep. She had always lain there, wide awake, thinking about what it would be like if it had been Zachary in bed with her.

Nathan's taunts that morning about her teasing Zachary all these years still stung, maybe because they were partially true. Yes, she *had* lived for the times she ran into Zachary at social functions, a reasonably frequent occurrence since he was the Whitmores' solicitor and a good friend of Byron's. She and Nathan had lived at Belleview during part of their marriage, and Zachary and his wife had come there often for dinner parties and other celebrations.

Lenore might have taken extra trouble with her appearance on those occasions. But she had never deliberately teased Zachary. Her only deliberate action was the one time she'd gone to his office, ostensibly to employ him in his professional capacity as a solicitor with one of her acting contracts. All she had wanted was to see him, not seduce him. Zachary, however, had treated her with such cool propriety that she hadn't gone through with that idea. He'd made her feel vaguely ashamed, as though it had been beneath her.

Yet she did so love him. He was more of a man than any man she'd ever known. Strong and gallant and good, and so handsome he made her go weak at the knees. He might be over forty now, but age had lent a broad-shouldered maturity to his super-tall frame and a dignity to his lean, angular face. He stood head and shoulders above most men in stature *and* character, in Lenore's opinion. Felicity didn't know how lucky she was to have such a man as her husband.

Felicity...

Lenore suppressed a sigh. If only Felicity weren't so damned pretty. And so damned delicate. Lenore sensed Zachary wasn't in love with his wife, but she could imagine a man's ego being constantly stroked by all that blonde, blue-eyed fragility. A lot of men liked the clingy, vulnerable variety of woman. Clearly, Zachary did.

'You've just driven straight past Belleview,' Kirsty said scornfully.

Lenore swore under her breath.

'Such language!' her daughter mocked.

Lenore's head snapped round to find her daughter grinning at her. When she grinned back, Kirsty's face began to crumple.

'I...I'm sorry, Mum,' she said in a strangled tone, 'I know I've been acting like a bitch. I don't know what's wrong with me.'

Lenore patted her daughter's bejeaned knee. 'It's all right, sweetie. I understand. I haven't been the best mother lately, either. Perhaps we both need some breathing space.'

'I'll try to be good for Dad.'

'I think that would be a wise idea. It was good of him to have you, you know. He's very busy at the moment with Byron still in hospital. If it hadn't been for the accident, he would have given up his position at Whitmore Opals to write full-time. For your information, Hollywood has just bought the rights to one of his boring old plays, so I wouldn't knock them if I were you. Your Dad happens to be a creative genius, my girl, and it's time you realised it.'

'Wow, Mum, do you realise you just stuck up for Dad? You still love him, don't you?'

Lenore sighed. 'Let's not get back to that, please. I couldn't stand it.'

By this time Lenore had negotiated a U-turn and they were approaching Belleview from the other direction. The clock on the dashboard showed eight, and the sun had just set.

'Do try to be pleasant to Melanie,' Lenore said pleadingly as they swung into the driveway. 'And don't make fun of Ava.'

'Melanie's a wet blanket and Ava's a dill. She *asks* to be made fun of.'

Lenore heaved another sigh and pointed the remote control at the gates.

'But I'll do my best,' Kirsty promised.

'Good. Oh, and one last thing. *No more smoking.*'

Kirsty turned an innocent-looking face towards her mother. 'Of course not. Smoking's bad for your health.'

'So's trying to con your father!'

Melanie came to greet them at the door, looking her usual prim and proper self with her black hair scraped back into a tight roll, no make-up on, and her figure disguised in a black shirtwaister uniform dress one size too large for her. Ghastly beige-coloured stockings and chunky black flatties completed the quite erroneous picture of a stodgy, boring, sexless woman the wrong side of thirty.

But there was no pretence in the dullness of her black eyes as she smiled her dead smile at both of them before taking Kirsty's bags. 'Hello, Kirsty...Lenore... I'll take these upstairs to your usual room, Kirsty. Nathan's waiting for you both in the billiard room, Lenore.'

Kirsty started walking ahead across the marble entry, under the huge semi-circular staircase and down the hallway that led down to the entertainment rooms.

'He—er—has someone with him,' Melanie told Lenore quietly as she went to follow her daughter.

The odd note in Melanie's voice stopped Lenore in her tracks. 'Wait a sec, Kirsty,' she called to her daughter. 'Who?' she asked, running her mind over Nathan's very few male friends and not coming up with anyone who would be playing billiards with him at eight o'clock on a Monday night.

'Her name's Gemma Smith,' the housekeeper said, throwing Lenore a look that was overly bland even for Melanie. It suggested something was up which was highly unusual.

Nathan had been seen around town with several women since his divorce. But he hadn't brought one home. Not to Belleview, anyway. This Gemma person had to be someone quite special.

But if Nathan was getting tangled up with some woman why hadn't he mentioned her this morning? And why had he invited Kirsty to live here with him if he had some female in tow? No way would Lenore condone Kirsty living here while her father was having it off with some blonde bimbo down the hall.

Lenore was shocked at her crude thoughts, and the undeniable stab of jealousy that had inspired them.

'Is there anything I should know about this Gemma?' she asked.

'Seeing is worth a thousand words,' Melanie said drily.

Lenore hurried on after Kirsty lest the girl get a nasty shock. Not that Lenore really thought Nathan would be making love to this Gemma on the billiard table when he was expecting his ex-wife and daughter to arrive at any moment. But it was better to be safe than sorry.

The billiard-room was the very last room on the left. Lenore caught up with Kirsty just as she reached the heavy wooden door which wasn't properly shut. The sounds of laughter came floating through the gap: light and musical and very, very young.

Lenore's eyes widened. Kirsty frowned over at her mother.

Unaccountably infuriated, Lenore pushed the door open without knocking, only to reveal the most astonishing sight.

Nathan was trying to teach a young woman in a pink sundress to play billiards. He was standing behind her— *close* behind her—and they were both bending over the table. Nathan's broad shoulders were wrapped around the girl's slender ones, his long arms extending to where he was showing her how to aim the cue stick.

'No, not like that,' he was saying. 'Slowly... Smoothly... You don't jab!'

'I'll never get the hang of it, Nathan. I'm a duffer. Oh!' she gasped, straightening abruptly when she saw Lenore standing in the open doorway. Nathan grunted from behind her.

Lenore's gaze swept over the girl, her already green eyes even greener with envy. What a beauty this gorgeous young creature was! Those eyes! And that figure! Why, her breasts were having trouble staying within the confines of that dress, yet her waist was so tiny a man like Nathan could put his hands right round it.

Her own eyes darted to her ex-husband, reproach replacing shock on her face. What, in God's name, was he doing with such a child? Why, the girl could be no more than seventeen or eighteen, only marginally older than his daughter. It was disgusting!

'And good evening to you too, Lenore,' Nathan drawled, coming out from behind the girl at long last. 'Come in, Kirsty,' he directed over Lenore's shoulder. 'I want you both to meet Gemma. She hails from Lightning Ridge and has just been employed as Whitmore Opals' newest salesgirl. Unfortunately, Byron won't let her start till she's done the mandatory Japanese course, but while she's doing that she'll be staying here at Belleview.'

'*What*?' Lenore exclaimed. But before she could launch into an argument with Nathan he cut her off.

'I've offered her a live-in position, keeping an eye on madam here before and after school, *and* at the week-end.'

'I don't need a babysitter!' Kirsty protested.

'Not a babysitter,' her father refuted. 'More of a minder. Which you *do* need, according to your mother. From what I hear, you're not doing your homework, you're being cheeky and you're smoking.'

Kirsty glared at her mother. 'Traitor,' she whispered fiercely.

'If this is an example of your manners, young lady,' Nathan said sternly, 'then I can see your mother was not exaggerating. Now say hello and goodbye to Gemma in one breath, then skedaddle off to your room. I'm sure you have some unpacking to do and your mother and I have some things to discuss with Gemma.'

Kirsty flounced off, muttering something about how *she* looked older than her minder. Which she almost did. At fourteen Kirsty was fully grown and developed, though her figure had a layer of puppy fat over it. By contrast, Gemma's face and body had fined down to those of a woman. It was only the way she was dressed and the way she did her hair that was trapping her age as an adolescent in other people's minds.

Nathan walked over and closed the door after Kirsty's grumbling departure. 'I see exactly what you mean,' he remarked to his ex-wife. 'But I still think it's a stage she's going through, nothing serious. What do you think, Gemma? You're closer to her in age than we are.'

'Which would have to be the understatement of the year,' Lenore muttered.

Nathan's look was scathing. 'Gemma happens to be twenty.'

'No, Nathan,' Gemma corrected, blushing prettily. '*Nearly* twenty.'

'How nearly?' Lenore snapped. 'The year 2000?'

'Oh, for pity's sake,' Nathan muttered.

Lenore rounded on him. 'Don't you "for pity's sake" me, Nathan Whitmore,' she spat at him. 'You come home with some strange girl I don't know from Eve and expect me to let her mind *my* daughter!'

'*Our* daughter, and I'll have you know that—'

'Please don't argue about me,' the girl interrupted in a quiet but surprisingly forceful dignity that Lenore had to admire. 'I... Mrs Whitmore is probably right, Nathan. This wasn't a good idea. Thank you so much for all your help but I think I should go to that motel you spoke of.'

'You will *not*!' Nathan pronounced with a passion that stunned Lenore.

Good God, if she didn't know better she might think he'd finally done the unthinkable—fallen in love.

'Lenore, I'm disappointed in you,' he swept on. 'You're usually a sensible clear-thinking woman. Do you honestly think I would bring someone into this home who wasn't above board? Besides, where's your Christian charity? The girl's mother is dead, her father died recently and she's all alone in the world. I met Gemma when I went to Lightning Ridge a few days back and promised to help her get on her feet if and when she came to Sydney. And I aim to do just that. If she can help us with Kirsty in return then so much the better.'

Lenore bit her tongue to stop herself from snapping back that since she wasn't a mind-reader she couldn't have been expected to know all that. She bestowed a less emotional, more assessing gaze on their visitor from Lightning Ridge and had to admit she liked the way the girl stood up straight and was studying her in return with unwavering eyes. There was integrity in her stance and honesty in her face. It was too bad that face was so lovely and that Nathan was obviously so susceptible to it.

'I'm sorry, Gemma,' she apologised drily. 'But you did come as rather a shock.'

'I understand, Mrs Whitmore. I have been rather shoved on to you without warning.' The girl smiled a softly sweet, but incredibly sensual smile that worried the hell out of Lenore. What man could resist *that*? She re-

solved to speak to Nathan privately, tell him that she
would not tolerate Kirsty being exposed to any kind of
Shenanigans. If he had to have this girl, then he could do
so somewhere else!

The thought of her ex-husband actually sleeping with
this innocent began to bother the life out of Lenore, yet
it didn't feel like jealousy any more. More like concern
for the girl. What was it about this creature that made
one warm to her on sight, made one want to protect her?

Perhaps she was misjudging Nathan. Maybe that was
what he felt too, an urge to protect.

And I'm Mahatma Gandhi, she told herself with rueful cynicism.

Lenore addressed both her ex-husband and his newly
found friend with a politeness she wasn't feeling.

'Maybe Gemma could go upstairs and get to know
Kirsty while I have a few words with you, Nathan.'

His sardonically arched eyebrow suggested he wasn't
fooled for a moment by Lenore's saccharine tone.

'Would that be all right with you, Gemma?' he asked
softly. 'Kirsty will be in the room right next to the one I
put you in.'

The girl smiled nervously up at him. 'Are...are you
sure about this, Nathan? I would hate to think I've
caused you any trouble. You're been so kind...'

Nathan actually took the girl's hands in his. 'Don't
trouble your pretty little head about a thing. It's time you
went upstairs anyway. You must be tired. You've had
quite a day.'

'Yes...Yes, I have.'

'I'm sorry about the opal, Gemma, but I was fairly
sure as soon as I saw it.'

Her sigh carried a weary resignation. 'I should have
known it was too good to be true.'

'I'll ask Byron again tomorrow about the reward. If it
hadn't been for that physiotherapist arriving, I would
have settled the matter this afternoon.'

'Tomorrow will do just as well,' the girl assured him,
their conversation totally confusing Lenore.

But she watched the interchange with growing interest. Nathan was different with this girl than any person she had ever seen him with, even his own daughter. Anyone not knowing Nathan might think he was acting in a fatherly fashion, but Lenore suspected it was nothing of the kind.

He coveted this girl, as one would a rare jewel. An opal, maybe, in its raw state. There was a glittering of suppressed passion in his eyes when he looked at her, as though he couldn't wait to get his hands on her, to strip away the superficial rough edges, to fashion and polish her till she was a priceless piece of art that all the world could see but only he could touch.

Lenore gave herself a mental shake. She was getting too fanciful for words. First thinking Nathan was in love, then this. She had to be going crazy. The Nathan she knew did not fall in love, or blindly covet, but he did have strong male needs. Which brought her right back to the problem at hand.

'It was nice meeting you, Mrs Whitmore,' the girl was saying and holding out her hand.

'And you, dear.' She briefly shook the proffered hand. 'But I think you should call me Lenore. Nathan gets peeved when people call me Mrs Whitmore these days.'

'I do not,' he growled.

'You do too.'

'Goodnight, Gemma,' he said curtly. 'Tell Kirsty I'll be up to see her after her mother has left.'

'All right. Goodnight again.'

'No wonder I'm having trouble with Kirsty's manners,' Nathan remarked testily once the sound of Gemma's departing footsteps receded.

Lenore was determined not to be side-tracked. 'Are you sleeping with that girl?'

She had never seen Nathan's eyes grow so cold. 'You would think that, wouldn't you?' He came forward to place a fingertip under her chin, tipping her face till her wide green eyes were staring into the wintry depths of his.

'Just because you can be had quite easily, Lenore, don't think every other woman is like that.'

Lenore gasped her hurt and would have spun away had not Nathan grasped her whole chin with his hand.

'What's the matter, darling?' he taunted in a low dangerous voice. 'Are you worried I'm getting something you're not? What's the matter, haven't you been able to seduce Zachary yet? Isn't your latest leading man coming across?'

'You're disgusting!' she exclaimed, and slapped his hand away.

Her action sent a wild fury into his face. Grabbing her by the shoulders, he yanked her hard against him, his mouth plummeting to take hers in a kiss of sheer spite and anger. Lenore struggled beneath its brutal onslaught but he seemed beside himself with an uncontrollable need to punish her for she knew not what. One of his hands slid round to grip her hair and he began pulling her head back so hard she thought her neck would break. Using her brains, she abruptly surrendered to his kiss, trying to defuse the situation by sighing and melting into him, opening her mouth to accept the violent thrusts of his tongue.

Neither of them saw the wide-eyed Gemma, standing just outside the open door, staring. She'd returned to get her cardigan from where she'd left it on a chair, only to be confronted with an oblivious Nathan kissing his ex-wife.

With a tortured groan, Gemma fled, her second departure going totally unnoticed.

CHAPTER FIVE

GEMMA ran blindly along the dimly lit hallway, tears stinging her eyes. God, what a fool she was. What a stupid, stupid fool!

Up the sweeping marble staircase she raced, intent on getting to her room where she could hide or cry or whatever. But as she turned right at the top of the stairs for the short dash down the hall to the guest bedroom Nathan had put her in, she crashed headlong into Ava.

Gemma had met Byron's 'kid' sister earlier that day, and she was the loveliest lady. They'd had afternoon tea together and a long chat, after which Gemma had happily accepted Nathan's offer of a live-in position at Belleview.

But the dear woman was carrying far too many pounds for her small-boned frame. So it was Ava who fell when Gemma collided with her, landing on her plump bottom and sliding across the marble-floored hallway to crash into the wall with a loud thud. A picture hanging on the wall above the point of impact was dislodged from its mounting and fell, just missing Ava's head. The corner of the gilt frame shattered as it hit the hard floor.

'Oh, dear,' Ava groaned, seemingly more concerned by the broken frame than her own physical condition. Gemma rushed over. 'I'm so sorry, Ava. Are you all right? I shouldn't have been running. I'm not usually so silly and clumsy. Here, let me help you up.'

It was a struggle to get Ava up on to her slippered feet which kept shooting out from under her. 'It's not you who's the clumsy one around here,' Ava said with an unhappy sigh. 'I fall over on average once a week. I'm just too fat!'

'You're not fat,' Gemma said kindly. 'You're pleasantly plump. And much as I think these marble floors are magnificent, they're also very slippery.'

Ava laughed, her bright blue eyes lighting up. It came to Gemma as she looked into Ava's round but pretty face that she would be extremely attractive if she lost a little weight and let her hair go back to the brown colour of her dark roots. That ginger frizz wouldn't have flattered any woman.

'How sweet of you to make excuses for me, but I *am* clumsy, and I also recently crossed the line from plump to fat. Why do you think I wear black pants and tent tops all the time? To hide the bulges!'

'What's happened?' came a sharp voice from behind them.

Gemma and Ava turned to see the housekeeper descending with a frown on her face. When they'd been introduced earlier that day, the woman had told Gemma to call her Melanie, but she preferred Mrs Lloyd. Melanie was far too warm a name for this frosty-faced martinet. She was a childless widow, Nathan had informed Gemma, who wondered again what man would ever marry such a coldly forbidding woman. No doubt the fictional Mrs Danvers Nathan had compared her with wasn't exactly a bundle of laughs, either.

'I...I'm afraid I've broken the frame of this picture, Melanie,' Ava said haltingly.

'Yes, so I see,' the woman answered in that monotone voice of hers, and picked the painting up from the floor. It was a landscape, reminiscent of the beautiful brush valley visible from the back windows of Belleview. St Ives was apparently on the fringes of Sydney—so Ava had enlightened Gemma—with a lot of national parks and reserves enhancing the much sought after locale.

'Please...don't tell Byron,' Ava said worriedly. 'I'll have it fixed before he comes home.'

'But it was all *my* fault,' Gemma protested. 'I was running up the stairs and I knocked into Ava. *I* should be the one to have the picture fixed.'

Melanie turned her deeply set black eyes Gemma's way, and Gemma could have sworn she saw surprise and respect in their usually expressionless depths.

'No, no,' Ava denied. 'It was clumsy me, as usual.'

'If Gemma says it was her fault then I believe her,' Melanie Lloyd pronounced firmly, then floored Gemma by smiling at her. It wasn't much of a smile, admittedly, a slight lifting of the corners of that thin-lipped mouth. But oh, the transformation to her face. Why, the woman was quite beautiful! And she didn't have thin lips at all!

'Byron makes adequate provision in the housekeeping money for simple breakages,' she advised. 'I'll see it's fixed and hanging back up well before he comes home from the hospital.'

'You're so efficient,' Ava praised with an envious-sounding sigh. 'I never seem to get anything done. I started a watercolour a few weeks ago and it's only half-way finished.'

'Speaking of getting things done, Ava,' the housekeeper said, 'do you think you could come downstairs and help me plan the dinner menus for the next week?'

'You want *my* help?' Ava looked shocked, but delighted.

'I certainly do. You have creative talent and I think the meals around here have become a little bland lately. I would value your suggestions.'

Ava fairly beamed, and Gemma smiled approval at the housekeeper. For a second their eyes locked, and a silent message passed between the two women. It bespoke an understanding that Ava was not as strong as they were, that she was a gentle creature who needed to be stroked and cosseted. All of a sudden, Gemma knew she would not think of the housekeeper as Mrs Lloyd any more. She would be Melanie from that moment on.

'I'll go and see how Kirsty is doing,' Gemma said.

'Yes,' Melanie agreed. 'I think that might be a good idea. Come along, Ava... We have work to do.'

Ava went off with Melanie quite happily, and Gemma turned to continue up the hall, the incident having provided a welcome interruption to the emotional breakdown she might have indulged in a few minutes before. Now, it seemed silly to burst into tears. Her misery was no less acute but her common sense had come to the rescue, making her see that it was a misery of her own making.

She'd been getting carried away all evening with Nathan's feeling towards her, misinterpreting his gallantry, mistaking his attentions in the billiard-room as the attentions of a man as smitten with her as she was with him. As if he would be!

The man was way out of her league, for heaven's sake. Years older in both age and experience. A man of the world. She'd been crazy to start thinking she could mean anything to him other than an amusing distraction. He would never fall in love with her. How could he? He was still in love with his ex-wife!

Gemma's stomach curled just thinking about that kiss she'd witnessed. She'd never seen anything like it. Such passion. Such intensity. Much as the memory pained her, she couldn't stop thinking about it, couldn't stop wondering why they had divorced if there was still such passion between them.

Gemma recalled Lenore's fury that morning as she'd stormed out of Nathan's office, how she'd called him impossible. Maybe they just hadn't been able to live together in harmony, maybe their personalities had not proved compatible. But it seemed there was one matter in which they were still highly compatible.

Tears hovered again, but Gemma steadfastly pushed them aside.

I wasn't really in love with him, she reasoned bravely. I was only infatuated. I'm not used to men like him with their city polish and their smooth charm. I lost my head for a minute, Ma, but it's back on again now, and I'm not about to lose it again in a hurry.

Gemma squared her shoulders and was continuing along the hallway when another thought had her grinding to a startled halt. Was a kiss—however passionate—proof of love?

Maybe not on Nathan's part, if Jade was to be believed about her adopted brother's cavalier treatment of women. Nathan had said not to believe a word Jade said, but what if she'd been telling the truth? What if...?

The possibility that her knight in shining armour was far from a saint in sexual matters crashed through Gemma, bringing dismay, but also a disturbing quickening of breath. She flushed to think of his supposed 'spur-of-the-moment' impulse to kiss her in the car. She had believed his excuse at the time.

But what if he'd been lying? What if he *had* brought her to Belleview to have his wicked way with her. Maybe not straight away, but eventually...

Gemma's head began to whirl, her pulse-rate picking up even further. She kept remembering how it had felt when Nathan had wrapped his body around hers at the billiard-table. At the same time she'd laughed in a vain attempt to relieve her blistering awareness of his hard flesh pressing into her soft buttocks, but in truth, she wouldn't—or couldn't—have stopped him from going further if he'd wanted to. Lenore and Kirsty had arrived in the nick of time.

But she couldn't always rely on someone arriving in the nick of time, could she?

Maybe she should clear right out. Leave Belleview.

Gemma frowned. But that would mean falling back on her own meagre resources in this enormous and extremely daunting city. She'd have to be insane to do that, to turn her back on this beautiful home, on a good job, and on the reward Nathan said Byron would give her. And she wasn't insane. Silly, maybe. And susceptible to a handsome face, as Ma had said. But she was learning, wasn't she? And now that her eyes were more open, she would be on the alert against being taken advantage of in any way. Given time, this infatuation or sexual attraction or whatever it was she felt for Nathan was sure to wane. Soon, she probably wouldn't even turn a hair when he came into the room!

Feeling slightly better, Gemma took the remaining steps that brought her to Kirsty's bedroom door, deciding she'd better get on with what she was being employed to do and break the ice with the girl. When there was no answer to her knock, she slowly turned the handle and peeped around the door. Kirsty was sitting, cross-legged, on her bed, puffing away on a cigarette.

The bold little hussy!

But neither Kirsty's defiant behaviour nor her smoking fazed Gemma. She'd been there, done that. Adopting an indifferent face, she walked right in, shutting the door behind her, then strode across the room where she flung open the window. 'Better get some air in here,' she said. 'Your dad will be up shortly and I don't think he'll want to smell smoke.'

Turning, she leant against the window-sill and looked around the room. It was a delight of femininity. All pink and white, with pink walls, off-white shag carpet, a white four-poster bed with a pink lace quilt and matching pink and white curtains at the windows. It was the sort of bedroom Gemma would have given her eye-teeth for while growing up—*any* bedroom would have done. But she suspected Kirsty hated its little-girl prettiness.

'God, this is frightful, isn't it?' Gemma remarked.

Kirsty blinked. 'Huh?'

'The room. It's frightful. We'll have to see what we can do to make it liveable-in.' Gemma levered herself away from the window and came over to take the cigarette out of Kirsty's suddenly slack mouth, taking a couple of puffs herself—to check for grass—before walking back and tossing it out of the window. 'Heck, Kirsty,' she said to the gaping girl, 'the least you could do is smoke a decent brand. That sucked.'

Kirsty was still staring at her when there was a tap tap on the door and Nathan strode in. Gemma was pleased to find she didn't go to mush, though her eyes did fly to his mouth. The bottom lip looked even fuller than usual—sort of soft and swollen and appallingly sexy. Gemma stiffened, her hands curling over the window-sill.

Nathan immediately sniffed the air. 'Do I smell smoke in here?' he growled.

Kirsty looked at Gemma, who shrugged. 'I can't smell anything.'

Nathan gave her a dry look. Gemma was now finding it hard to look him straight in the face without thinking about the last time she'd seen him, with a moaning Lenore in his arms.

Yanking her mind back from that path, she lifted her chin and launched into another minefield—winning Kirsty over. 'One thing I wanted to ask you, Nathan,' she said in an amazingly steady voice. *See*, she told herself. Progress already.

'Yes?' Nathan said curtly.

'Would Kirsty and I be able to redecorate this room? Pink and white lace is rather babyish for a fourteen-year-old. I do realise this is Byron's home, but...'

'Oh, *please*, Dad,' Kirsty joined in. 'I won't change it too much. Just a few posters and stuff.'

He sighed. 'All right, provided you clear it with Melanie. She's in charge of the house.'

Kirsty's face fell. 'That miserable bitch.'

'*Kirsty*!' both Nathan and Gemma chorused at once.

'Well, she *is*,' Kirsty insisted sulkily.

'You wouldn't feel like laughing all the time if you saw your husband and only child incinerated in a car accident,' Nathan berated his daughter. 'It's a wonder the woman's still sane, let alone a functioning human being.'

Both Kirsty and Gemma gaped at him in shock.

'Gee,' Kirsty said at last. 'That sucks.'

Nathan gave his daughter another reproachful look. 'Maybe you'll look for the reason behind a person's behaviour before you make a judgement next time, madam. And please don't use that expression. I find it offensive.'

'What? Sucks? Gemma said it earlier, so why can't I?'

Nathan swung surprised eyes her way.

Gemma cringed inside but kept her chin up.

'Has Mum gone home?' Kirsty said. 'Why didn't she come and say goodbye?'

'She said she'd call you as soon as she got home.'

The telephone beside the bed started ringing at exactly that moment.

'That'll be your mother now.'

Kirsty snatched up the receiver. 'Mum? Hi there. No, it's OK. I didn't mind. Gemma and I have been getting to know each other. Yeah, I think so. She's real cool...' And she flashed Gemma a wide smile.

Gemma smiled back, feeling pleased with herself. But when Nathan gestured brusquely for her to come out into the hall with him, everything inside her tensed. No doubt he was only going to haul her over the coals for encouraging his daughter to use such language, but she still didn't want to be alone with him. Her susceptibility hadn't waned yet, not even a little bit.

'I don't know how you've managed it so quickly,' Nathan started once the bedroom door was safely closed, 'but Melanie speaks highly of you, Ava thinks you're a darling and my difficult daughter actually seems to *like* you. Care to tell me your secret?'

'I don't think I have any secret,' she returned tautly. 'Mostly, I just try to be myself.'

His smile was wry. 'How come I don't think the Gemma Smith I've come to know and respect would use an expression such as something "sucks"?'

Gemma felt a smile tugging at her lips. 'When in Rome, do as the Romans do.'

'Aah...and are you going to take up smoking as well?'

Now she laughed, her tension easing. 'Maybe,' she admitted. 'For a while.'

'And the room? Will I have to gird myself the next time I dare to enter?'

'Definitely.'

'Should I accept anything and everything with po-faced indifference?'

'Good heavens, no. Kirsty would be disappointed if you did that. You have to cringe and say how simply ghastly it all is. What would be the fun if your parents accepted the way you did up your room?'

'Oh? And did *your* father cringe at the way you did up your room when you were a teenager?'

Gemma flinched at the mention of her father. 'I didn't have a room of my own, for starters,' came her bleak reply. 'And I'm still a teenager,' she reminded him pointedly.

Nathan frowned. 'So you are, Gemma. So you are. One day, perhaps, you might like to tell me all about your life at Lightning Ridge, and your father. I realise that with his death being so recent you might not want to talk about him right now, but I would like to know what events made you into the woman you are today. And before you say differently, you *are* a woman, not a teenager. You're as far removed from Kirsty as night is from day.'

Gemma felt uncomfortable with his saying such flattering things about her. She was also uncomfortable with the way his eyes started travelling down her face and neck to where her breasts were rising and falling in an uneven rhythm.

Fear curled her stomach. Not so much of him, but of herself. All of a sudden, she wanted to be in his arms as Lenore had been, wanted him to do what she had stopped him doing in the car. She couldn't stop looking at his mouth, his lovely full-lipped mouth. The yearning to have that mouth on hers was so sharp she almost moaned.

'I . . . I must be going to bed,' she blurted out instead. 'I'm very tired.'

His eyes lifted, and while they looked cool enough, she suspected their owner wasn't. There was a stillness about him that made her hold her breath, that sent her eyes flaring with wide apprehension. The air around them seemed to crackle with a dark electricity which felt both ominous and threatening.

Don't, she screamed silently at him with an internal panic close to hysteria. *Please* don't...

'Did Melanie tell you the arrangements we have here for breakfast?' he said, his voice clipped.

Gemma nodded, unable to find her voice.

'Fine. Would seven-thirty be too early for you to meet me in the morning-room?'

'No,' she croaked.

'Good. I'd like to discuss a few things with you before I go to work. I'll see you at seven-thirty, then. Goodnight, Gemma. Sweet dreams.'

She watched him walk away, aware that she had started to shake. Sweet dreams? The man was mad, or bad, or both!

When Gemma presented herself in the morning-room at seven-thirty the following morning, Nathan was sitting at the oval-shaped breakfast table, an empty coffee-cup in front of him, his face buried in the morning paper. Any other time, Gemma would have turned to admire the room with its cool green walls, attractive cane furniture and wide picture windows through which the morning sun was streaming. But her attention was riveted on the top of that gleaming golden head as she waited, breathless, for the moment those grey eyes would lift and notice her standing there.

But it was Melanie, gliding in to top up Nathan's coffee, who spied her first and said good morning. Only then did Nathan glance up, his gaze unreadable as it rapidly surveyed her from top to toe then back again. Her simple floral dress with its dropped waist and tiny white buttons down the front was cheap, price-wise, as were all her clothes, but it was fairly new, the cotton material still crisp, the cream and apricot colours suiting her dark hair and olive complexion. The brown leather sandals on her bare feet were real leather, a gift from Ma at Christmas.

It was her hair, however, that seemed to hold Nathan's eyes for an extra moment or two, her thick dark wavy hair which she'd left down this time to curl gently around her face and shoulders.

'Good morning, Gemma,' he said, folding the newspaper crisply and placing it on the table beside his now full coffee-cup. 'You're looking refreshed this morning. I trust you slept well?'

She had, surprisingly, maybe from sheer exhaustion, or because her bed was so comfortable.

'I did,' she said stiffly, and came forward, determined to conquer this spell he seemed to have cast over her. It wasn't love, she'd reasoned again on waking. But it *was* powerfully disturbing.

When she hesitated over which chair to sit in, Nathan made up her mind for her by pulling out the one nearest his right. She sat down, noting ruefully that not all the common sense resolutions in the world could control her wildly beating heart in his presence, nor stop herself from staring at him all the time.

But he was just so handsome. And sleek. And polished. And *clean*!

She was used to men stinking of stale sweat and body odour, their hands and nails thick with grime, their clothes looking as if they hadn't been washed in a month. Which they probably hadn't.

Nathan sat there, his freshly shampooed hair gleaming in the sunlight, no stubble on his just-shaven jaw, his broad-shouldered body elegantly encased in a pale grey three-piece suit that didn't know the word 'crease'.

Gemma could have sat there forever, drinking in his beauty, her nostrils being pleasantly teased by his pine-scented aftershave, had Melanie not asked, 'What would you like for breakfast, Gemma?'

Now, Gemma had never in her life had anyone ask her that question before. Last night at dinner she'd been in awe of Melanie's home-made celery soup, mouthwatering steak and salad, and custard cake afterwards. But that meal had simply been placed in front of her. She hadn't been required to make a choice.

'Oh . . . I—er . . .'

'Bring her the same as I had,' Nathan intervened, much to Gemma's relief.

'Coming right up,' Melanie said briskly, and departed through a sliding door which Gemma presumed led into the kitchen. Ava had given her a tour of the house yesterday but they'd missed some sections when Ava had suddenly decided to take Gemma back upstairs and show their new visitor her watercolours.

'You must be a little nonplussed over all that's happened to you this past week,' Nathan remarked thoughtfully as he lifted the coffee-cup to his mouth.

Gemma didn't know what to say to that. What did nonplussed mean? 'Er—yes, I am,' she agreed. When in doubt, always agree with one's elders or betters. Another one of Ma's pearls of wisdom.

'I just realised this morning I hadn't even enquired about what you've been doing with yourself since you left school.'

'Not a lot,' she admitted. 'The only work I could find around Lightning Ridge was some part-time waitressing in a café. I wanted to go to Walgett to find work but my father wouldn't let me.'

'I see . . . And what were you like at school?'

'Average, I suppose. I didn't set the world on fire with my HSC marks but I was sick with glandular fever at the time of the exams.'

'Ah . . . the kissing disease . . .'

'The what?'

'Glandular fever is sometimes called the kissing disease. It races through high school and colleges because it's easily passed on by kissing.'

'Well, it wasn't passed on to *me* that way.'

Gemma found herself on the end of an intense look from Nathan which might have truly flustered her if Kirsty hadn't dashed into the room at that moment. She was still in her dressing-gown and looked as if she'd just jumped out of bed.

'Gosh, Dad, I'm running late. Nobody got me up and I haven't even had a shower yet. Can you drive me to school when I'm ready?'

'Firstly, madam,' her father returned sternly, 'nobody around here is going to get you up of a morning. You're old enough to take some responsibility for your own life. You have a radio beside your bed with a built-in alarm. Set it before you go to sleep in future and when it goes off, get up! Secondly, I am not driving you to school. I have to leave for the office in a couple of minutes or I'll be late. Gemma will drive you to school, *and* pick you up this afternoon. And one last thing before you go. I don't want to hear you weren't wearing your proper uniform, which also means no jewellery and no make-up. Is that clear?'

'You're worse than Mum!' Kirsty wailed as she flounced out.

'I'm bigger too,' he called after her, then turned to grin at Gemma before seeing how pale and panicky she looked.

'What have I said?' he asked, frowning. 'You do drive, don't you? You did out at Lightning Ridge. Ava has said you can borrow her car. It's small and automatic. Very easy to handle.'

'It's not the driving part that worries me,' Gemma croaked. 'It's the traffic!'

'Oh, you don't have to take her into the city,' Nathan said dismissively. 'Kirsty's school is only a few miles up the road. Not far at all. The traffic's light around here. Look, I have to away.'

'But... but... what will I do for the rest of the day?'

He frowned. 'Never had the problem of telling a woman how to spend her day. I have no idea. Read a book. Watch television. Go shopping. Keep Ava company. I don't know. Ask Melanie. She'll know what you can do. Perhaps you could start planning what horrors you're going to perpetrate on that bedroom. You've probably only got this week to do that. Come next Monday you'll be fully occupied learning Japanese.'

He stood up, reminding Gemma how tall he was. Her neck crinked as she looked up at him.

'Will Ava be up before it's time for me to take Kirsty?' she asked worriedly.

'Should be. If not, Melanie keeps a spare set of keys to all the cars. Ask her. Oh, and there's a Gregory's Guide in the glove-box of the car in case you get lost.'

Gemma couldn't help a small groan.

Nathan's hand curved over her shoulder in what she supposed was a comforting gesture, but Gemma's immediate reaction to his touch was not comfort. Everything tightened inside her and she dropped her eyes away from his, lest he see her instant tension.

'You'll be all right,' he said. 'I have every confidence in your abilities to cope with anything life can throw at you.'

Something in his voice drew her to glance up.

It was a mistake. For his eyes fastened on to hers and in no time she was drowning ... drowning ...

Through a swirling haze she heard him mutter something, saw his eyes darken and narrow, saw his head begin to descend. Her lips gasped softly apart in anticipation of feeling his mouth on hers, but at the last moment he didn't kiss her. He straightened, lancing her with a savage look while adjusting his tie and doing up his suit jacket.

'Let me give you a little bit of advice, Gemma,' he warned darkly. 'If it's your intention to keep me at a distance, then do not look at me like you did just then. Take a leaf out of Melanie's book! She's mastered the art of freezing any man's desire at a single glance.'

He exited the room with long, angry strides, leaving Gemma to stare after him with a flushed face and madly thudding heart. She didn't hear Melanie come in with her breakfast, so she almost jumped out of her skin when the woman spoke.

'Nathan's a very handsome man, isn't he?' she commented coolly as she placed the plate of scrambled eggs before Gemma. 'Has women throwing themselves at him all the time.'

Gemma looked up into Melanie's intelligent dark eyes. 'Watch yourself with him,' the housekeeper said in a hard voice. 'He's trouble.'

CHAPTER SIX

LENORE couldn't believe any of it. First, that Kirsty had invited her to come over and see what she had been allowed to do to her bedroom, then that Melanie had actually *allowed* her and Gemma to turn the previously pretty room into such an eye-popping horror.

Kirsty stood there, giggling, while Lenore's wide gaze took in the never-ending posters, all of them seemingly of the one male pop singer who had sleepy dark eyes and a perpetually sulky mouth. Since the name 'Johnny' appeared with regularly monotony, she assumed that was his name.

The black and white poster wallpaper was only part of it, however, the lovely lace bedspread having been replaced by a black and white geometric print throwover that made one's eyes water just looking at it. The only consolation was that they hadn't hung matching curtains at the window. There were *no* curtains at the window, she suddenly realised.

'Get real, Mum,' Kirsty said when Lenore mentioned this. 'Curtains suck.'

Lenore groaned and threw an anguished look at Gemma who mouthed for her to 'stay cool'.

'Melanie and I put the curtains and quilt carefully away,' she whispered when Kirsty was preoccupied raving over her favourite poster. 'The posters are attached with a special glue-tack that comes off easily. Nothing's been done that can't be undone in a day.'

Lenore was beginning to feel a grudging respect for this girl. She'd been surprised when she arrived at Belleview today to find that Nathan had taken himself off for the weekend to his beach-house at Avoca—*alone*. Apparently, he'd extended an invitation for the two girls to go with him, but Gemma, it seemed, had been the one to talk Kirsty into staying behind to finish redecorating the room. This was hardly the action of a girl with her eye on snaring the highly eligible Nathan Whitmore for herself.

Still, Lenore was in no doubt that Gemma found Nathan very very attractive. It had been in her eyes the other night whenever she looked at him. Nathan hadn't been much better. He'd been drooling with desire, though he tried not to show it.

Not that he would have any intention of *marrying* the girl. He'd vowed after their divorce that he would never marry or have children again. No, Nathan would have a less permanent position in mind for this breathtakingly lovely creature. God, just look at her! How many girls could look a million dollars in that cheap little dress she was wearing? *And* without a scrap of make-up. What she could look like in the right clothes and with the right make-up was anyone's guess.

But perhaps it was her very ingenuousness that was bewitching Nathan. Maybe, like a lot of men, he harboured the fantasy of taking a beautiful but innocent virgin and moulding her into the perfect sexual partner for himself. He would teach her how to please him in every way. Yes, she could imagine that fantasy appealing to Nathan very much. He didn't hold a high opinion of women in general, especially ones of the more experienced kind. A virgin would suit him very well. And Gemma, unless she was severely mistaken, was just that!

A wry smile hovered round Lenore's lips as she pretended to look at the various posters. She could well imagine Nathan's irritation that his plans for Gemma were being side-lined by the girl herself. Lenore didn't believe his angry assertions the other night that his helping her had been a gesture of Christian charity. If it was, it was the first time Nathan had played Good Samaritan.

No, there had to be another reason for his sudden interest in the girl, and Lenore knew exactly what that reason was. His totally unexpected but explosive kiss the other night was very telling. Nathan, it seemed, was in a state of high sexual frustration. Thank God he'd quickly got a hold of himself on that occasion or she might eventually have been forced to kick him.

Hopefully, for Gemma's sake, he would pick up some willing little floozy this weekend up at Avoca and rid himself of all that tension. There were always plenty of beach bunnies hanging around on the weekends, and Nathan, in swimming-trunks, was an enticing sight. Golden Greek gods never had any trouble finding women to satisfy their sexual needs, especially when they didn't have a conscience to get in the way.

Lenore's mind drifted inevitably to Zachary Marsden and she sighed.

'I know this isn't your style, Mum,' Kirsty said quite happily, 'but I think it's awesome.'

Lenore turned to her daughter and smiled. 'I'm happy if you're happy, sweetie.'

'Are you? Great. Then can I have twenty dollars to go to a blue-light disco tonight? It's at the school hall and I'll be *real* happy if I can go.'

Lenore frowned. She'd grounded Kirsty for a month less than two weeks ago. Would her daughter think her weak if she gave in? Damn it all, this was the kind of problem she'd hoped Nathan could solve for a while. That man hadn't changed. He was still as selfish as ever. He had no business going off for the weekend and leaving Kirsty behind. He should have *insisted* she go with him.

'I think not, Kirsty,' she said.

'Oh, *Mum*!'

'You know you're grounded for another two weeks.'

'Yes, but that was *before* . . .'

'Before what?'

'Before I came to live here. Before Gemma. She'll take me and pick me up, right outside the door. She knows her

way around now,' Kirsty laughed. 'She got lost last
Tuesday, though, didn't you Gemma?'

Suppressing a jab of very real jealousy, Lenore turned
to face Gemma, who gave her an understanding smile.

'I think, Kirsty,' Gemma said in her melodic but surprisingly mature voice, 'that if you've been grounded,
you shouldn't be asking your mother to go back on her
word. We can just as easily get some videos and enjoy
ourselves here at home.'

'Yeah, I suppose that would be just as good, provided
we can get some funny ones. None of that serious stuff.'

'Do you think I could stay and watch them with you?'
Lenore asked, not happy with feeling left out of her
daughter's life, which was crazy since a couple of days
ago she'd been happy to get rid of her for a while.

'Sure thing, Mum.' Kirsty beamed and gave her a hug.
'We'll have a ladies' night. We'll even invite Ava.'

'What about Melanie?' Gemma suggested.

Lenore frowned. 'I don't think Kirsty likes Melanie
much.'

'No, Mum, I was wrong about Melanie. She's not too
bad.'

Lenore blinked over at her daughter.

'Did you know about what happened to her family,
Mum? I suppose you must have since Dad knew. He told
Gemma and me about it and boy, were we shocked!'

'It *was* a shocking thing,' Lenore agreed, 'but for
heaven's sake don't mention it in front of Melanie. She's
trying to forget it.'

'She must be a very brave lady,' Gemma murmured.

'Yes, I think so,' Lenore agreed. 'But even the bravest
of us have breaking points...' Once again, her mind
drifted to Zachary and she felt the most awful pain in her
heart. How long, she thought, before *my* breaking point
comes, how long before I go to him and make an utter
fool of myself again?

Tears pricked at her eyes and she just managed to stop
them gathering force.

'I'll tell you what,' she said with false brightness. 'How about we go and visit Byron in hospital this afternoon, then we can pick up the videos on the way home? I haven't been to visit him since just after his accident and I've been feeling guilty. Have you met Byron yet, Gemma?'

The girl looked startled and a fraction worried by the suggestion. 'N...no. But surely he won't want to see me from his hospital bed. I'm not family.'

'Neither am I, strictly. What do you call an ex-daughter-in-law of an adopted father?'

'A right pain in the bum,' Kirsty giggled. 'Now Mum, don't deny it. That's what Pops said you were when you wanted to go back to acting and Dad didn't want you to.'

Lenore sighed. 'Byron's a dear man,' she explained to Gemma, 'but he thinks a woman's place is firmly in the home. But I won't hold that against him today. He's got his own problems now and I'm sure meeting you would give him a lift. You must know a lot about opals, coming from Lightning Ridge, and opals are his greatest passion!'

Gemma stayed just inside the door, feeling awkward and embarrassed. The man propped up in the big white bed in the private hospital room was a formidable figure, and exactly as Ma had described. Very handsome for a man of his age, with thick black hair going grey at the temples, piercing blue eyes which missed nothing and a mouth that stood for no nonsense.

'What are you doing skulking over there, girl?' he said in his deep rumbly voice. 'Come over here where I can get a good look at you; have to see what's impressed my family so much. All I heard from Ava this past week was "Gemma this" and "Gemma that".'

Gemma didn't miss the slight raising of his eyebrows as she walked forward, nor the way those incisive blue eyes encompassed her thoroughly with one sweeping glance. 'You're certainly a good-looking girl, I'll say that for you. And you're twenty, Nathan tells me?'

'*Nearly* twenty,' Lenore corrected in a tone that brought a sharp look from Byron.

'I wasn't talking to you, Lenore.'

'Pardon me for breathing,' she said without turning a hair. Gemma received the impression that these two rather enjoyed sparring with each other. There'd already been several caustic interchanges since they'd arrived.

'It's been sweet of you to come and visit me, Lenore, but why don't you take yourself and Kirsty down to the cafeteria for a coffee?' he suggested. 'It's down the end of the corridor. I have some business I wish to discuss with Gemma here. In private.'

Gemma felt awful at Lenore and Kirsty being summarily dismissed like that, though they didn't seem to mind. Kirsty especially had been clearly bored by the visit. But seeing them disappear down the corridor increased the butterflies in her stomach. Byron Whitmore was an intimidating man who, despite Ma's glowing reference, radiated an aura of ruthless power. She admired Lenore for the way she stood up to him.

'Right,' he began sternly straight away. 'Now tell me how you think the Heart of Fire came to be in your father's possession?'

'The... the Heart of Fire?'

'The black opal, girl. It was named that by my father over fifty years ago. What do you think I'm talking about, a romance novel? Now there's no need to look like that. My bark's worse than my bite. I'm not accusing your father of anything criminal. He might have been an innocent dupe in all this. Just tell me what you know.'

Gemma stared at Byron, her mind ticking over with his words. An innocent dupe... Maybe her father hadn't been a thief at all. Maybe someone gave him the opal. Or maybe he simply found it somewhere.

'Well, girl? Speak up. If you're to work behind the counter of one of my stores you'd better get rid of that shyness of yours.'

Gemma's eyes flashed and her chin shot up. 'I'm not shy,' she denied. 'I was thinking.'

'By gum, she has spirit as well. Nathan can certainly pick them. Tell me what you were thinking.'

His reference to Nathan distracted her for a second, but with those blue eyes boring into her Gemma quickly regrouped her thoughts and told him the little she knew.

'So, in fact, you know nothing!' Byron announced, clearly disappointed.

'I'm afraid so.'

'Ah, well, maybe it's all for the best,' he grumbled. 'That opal's brought nothing but bad luck. I think I'll have it cut up into several smaller stones and be done with the damned thing.'

'*What*?' Gemma saw red, and when she saw red, she said things that perhaps were better left unsaid. But she never thought of that till afterwards. 'I would have expected more from an opal man than to hold with that old wives' tale about opals bringing bad luck,' she burst out. 'You must know that garbage was put around by diamond traders because they were scared people would start buying opals instead of diamonds. And why wouldn't they? They're far more beautiful. As for cutting up that magnificent stone...'

She drew herself up straight with righteous indignation. 'I can't think of a worse travesty against mother nature. An opal like that doesn't come along very often and its beauty should be protected for posterity, not desecrated. Now I see that my father had the right idea, keeping such a precious prize hidden away like that. Maybe he knew once he surrendered it to someone like you it would be gone forever!'

Her tirade finished, Gemma found that, as was usually the case, her anger dissipated quickly, to be replaced with horror that she had spoken in such a way to her employer.

'Oh,' she said, her face crumpling with remorse. 'Oh, dear...'

Byron's laughter was a surprise and a relief. 'Don't stop now,' he chuckled. 'I haven't had such a good dressing-down in years. You'd make even the matron around here sit up and take notice when your blood is up, girl. You'll make a damned good seller of opals, I'll warrant. You have a passion for them that's truly rare. Yes, rare...' He seemed to be mulling something over in his mind before saying unexpectedly, 'You're an orphan, is that right?'

'Y... yes.'

'Mmm. The reward... You thought it fair?'

Gemma recalled her shock when Nathan told her Byron was giving her a hundred thousand dollars, invested for her in a secure bank account till she decided what she wanted to do with it. She still couldn't comprehend the amount.

'You've been more than generous,' she said.

'It'll provide a deposit for a roof over your head if you ever need it.'

She frowned. 'Only a deposit?' That amount would have bought her a whole house and land out at the Ridge.

'This is Sydney, my dear, the dearest place in Australia to live. But you don't have to worry about where to live for now. You're staying at Belleview for the time being, aren't you?'

'Yes.'

'It'll be good for Kirsty to have someone nearer her own age around.'

'She's a nice kid.'

'Yes, I think so too. Still upset, though, over her parents' divorce. A bad thing, divorce...'

'Maybe Nathan and Lenore will get back together again,' Gemma said.

Byron gave her an odd look. 'No, I don't think so. Not now...'

'That's a shame.'

'Oh, I don't know about that. Lenore never was the right woman for Nathan. Too ambitious. He needs a girl who will devote herself to him and his needs, not crave for her own moon and stars all the time. Call me old-fashioned, but I think most men want that. If more women stayed home and looked after their families there would be fewer divorces.'

Gemma refrained from making comment. She'd already said enough, she thought. But she didn't agree with Byron. Women were better educated now and there was no way they could live the lives their grandmothers had led and not feel bored and unfulfilled. Sure, they had obligations to their families, if they had them, but they had obligations to themselves as well. They were people too, weren't they, with needs and desires of their own? They had a right to careers if that was what they wanted and, if husbands understood and supported them in that, *then* there would be fewer divorces.

But Gemma resisted saying so. Instead she studied the man in the bed and wondered if his poor dead wife had stayed home and if she'd been happy. Privately, Gemma didn't think being married to Byron Whitmore would be a recipe for happiness, despite all his money. He was far too bossy, not to mention chauvinistic. As for his opinion on Lenore and Nathan getting back together again... well, maybe she knew something Byron didn't know...

'We've finished our coffee,' Lenore announced from the doorway. 'Have you finished talking business yet, Byron? Because if you have, we must away.'

'Yes, we're finished.' Byron bestowed a softer, more charming goodbye smile on Gemma which showed another side to his personality. She suspected he'd been quite a one with the ladies over the years. 'Nice meeting you at last, Gemma. And good luck with your Japanese lessons. I want to see you behind that counter selling opals for Whitmore's as soon as possible. Er—could I have a quick word with you, Lenore, before you go? *Alone.*'

Lenore frowned, then handed Kirsty her car keys with a resigned sigh. 'You and Gemma wait for me at the car. I'll try not to be long.

'Well, what is it?' she asked as soon as the others were out of earshot. 'If you're going to go on about Nathan and me again you're wasting your time.'

'I realise that. I have a favour to ask of you.'

'Oh, yes?' Lenore's tone was wary. She didn't trust Byron, whom she considered a tyrant of the first order. He meant well but he liked trying to run other people's lives because he thought he knew best. But his standards were impossibly high and no one could live up to them. It was no wonder that his own daughter, Jade, had gone wild after she came of age and inherited her own money. She'd had twenty-one years of strict discipline and stupidly old-fashioned ideas shoved down her throat. Only Ava had completely given in to Byron's tyranny, and just look at her, the poor thing. Stripped of every ounce of confidence and self-esteem, waiting for some mythical Prince Charming to sweep into her life and make her happy. As if any man could make Ava happy. Didn't she know she had to be happy with herself first?

'I want you to help that Gemma girl with her wardrobe,' Byron said. 'Get her to buy some decent suits and blouses that would be suitable for work. And some other clothes as well. Casual, as well as dressy. And do something with her hair. Have it cut. Not short, but shaped properly around her face. And teach her to apply make-up without it seeming overdone. You know what I mean. Give her some class.'

'I think Nathan likes Gemma the way she is,' Lenore said drily.

Byron's eyes snapped to hers. 'So! You've seen the attraction for yourself, have you? What is this, Lenore? You don't want Nathan but you don't want anyone else to have him?'

'She's only a child,' Lenore muttered, still struggling with how she felt when she thought of Nathan really wanting another woman. Maybe he hadn't loved *her*, but he had desired her. Often.

'Only in superficial ways,' Byron argued, 'and you're going to fix one of those.'

'What makes you think I'll do what you ask? And if I do, what makes you sure I won't deliberately make her look awful?'

Byron's smile was smug. 'Because I'm going to bribe you not to.'

'How?' she scoffed. 'I have enough money of my own from the divorce settlement.'

'Have you read Nathan's new play?'

Lenore frowned. What was the conniving devil getting at now? 'Nathan doesn't show me his work any more,' she said coldly.

'It's very good.'

'I'm sure it is.'

'I'm going to invest in it. In fact, I'll be the only investor.'

'So?'

'It has a marvellous part in it for a woman. A beautiful woman of around your age...'

Lenore tried to contain her excitement. A lead role in one of Nathan's plays would set her on the road to real success. But Nathan would never give her the part.

'You...you'd suggest me for the role?'

'I'd insist you have it.'

'You're a wicked man.'

'I want Nathan to be happy, and, contrary to popular opinion, I want you to be happy too. Well, what do you say?'

'A makeover takes money, Byron. I might have enough but I'm not spending my own money starting up a new girlfriend for my ex-husband.'

'The girl has plenty of money herself.'

'Does she? How come?'

'I gave it to her for an opal that had come into her possession.'

'Well, well. OK, Byron, it's a deal. But has it occurred to you that Nathan won't marry this girl? He might just want her for sex.'

'Yes,' he surprised her by saying. 'But that's all right with me, if it makes him happy.'

'You shock me, Byron.'

'I almost died a few weeks ago, Lenore. Irene did die. Death has a way of making one reassess one's life and attitudes. I've been a fool in more ways than one but I mean to be different from now on.'

'How? By bribing me and poking your nose into Nathan's private life? You haven't really changed, Byron. You've merely changed your objectives. But no sweat. I'll do what you ask and God help you if you don't come through with your promise of that part. But I'll be giving Gemma some subtle warnings along the way. Because Nathan hasn't changed either. I have no intention of leading another lamb to the slaughter!'

Lenore spun on her high heels and strode quite angrily from the room. She marched down the highly polished hall, thumped the 'down' arrow of the lifts and was waiting there, fuming in silence, when the lift doors shot open and Zachary Marsden stepped out.

CHAPTER SEVEN

LENORE stared at him for a long, excruciatingly heartaching moment, seeing nothing but the glittering lights of pleasure that danced in his midnight-blue eyes before he could stop them.

He's glad to see me, she thought with a wild rush of overwhelming joy.

But no sooner had she thought that than Zachary schooled his face once again into the mask of cool politeness he always adopted whenever he met her.

'Lenore,' he said with a small incline of his head, making no attempt to shake her hand in any way, or give her a kiss on the cheek. Yet it had been over two years since they'd seen each other, Lenore's divorce from Nathan having cut their social ties.

'Zachary,' she returned, ignoring the lift behind her, which eventually shut its doors and moved on.

How marvellous he looks, she was thinking as she stood there, his very male body encased in dark blue trousers and a pale blue short-sleeved golfing shirt. She was used to seeing him in business or dinner suits, not casual clothes, but it was clear that Zachary had kept his forty-five-year-old body in great shape. Perhaps he'd come to the hospital straight from the golf-course, because his normally neat and tidy thick brown hair was windblown, and there was a faint sheen of sweat on his high forehead that bespoke physical activity.

'I've come to see Byron,' he said brusquely.

'I've just left him.'

'Really? I'm surprised. You and he were never the best of friends.'

Lenore shrugged, her earlier fury with Byron seeming inconsequential now. All that mattered at this moment was finding some excuse to stay and talk to Zachary. Yet the girls were waiting for her in the car and it was so hot out in the open-air car park. She hoped they'd thought to turn on the engine and the air-conditioning!

'You're looking well, Lenore,' Zachary remarked, his eyes sweeping down over her own very casual outfit of apricot bermuda shorts and matching T-shirt. 'Divorce obviously agrees with you. How's Kirsty?' he added pointedly. 'I'd be surprised if she's as happy with the situation.'

Hurt by his sarcasm—and perhaps stung by guilt over Kirsty—Lenore lied outrageously. 'Kirsty's fine. She's not a little girl any more, Zachary. She's fourteen. Quite old enough to understand that her father and I were not happy together. Besides, it wasn't a bitter divorce. Nathan and I are still good friends. She's living with him at the moment in fact, at Belleview.'

'How very civilised of you,' Zachary drawled. 'Pity *all* people can't get over the pain of divorce so easily.'

Lenore looked away from his brittle blue eyes. How quickly her pleasure at seeing Zachary again had vanished. He was still the same man. Still inflexible in matters of morals and marriage, still intolerant of human failings. Didn't he know that not everyone was as strong as he was?

The lift doors opened again and people stepped out. Zachary and Lenore moved to one side to let them pass along the corridor.

'I haven't seen your name up in lights lately,' Zachary resumed. 'Are you still acting?'

'Yes. I start rehearsal next week for a new play. It's a comedy of manners. A real farce.'

'You usually go in for drama, don't you, not farce?'

Lenore shrugged. Her whole life felt like a farce right at that moment. Why was she making chillingly polite conversation with this man when what she wanted was to throw herself into his arms and tell him how much he meant to her, had always meant to her? For all she knew, he might think she'd *loved* Nathan when she married him, that she'd forgotten *him* as quickly as her actions had made it seem.

But she'd never forgotten him, never stopped loving him, right from the first moment she'd seen him nearly fifteen years ago, when she'd been a nineteen-year-old fledgling actress, and he'd been a thirty-year-old rising star of a solicitor.

Lenore had just won a small role in the first play Nathan had written. Zachary, as a friend and business colleague of Byron's, had put up some of the money for the production, and had dropped in at rehearsals one day to see how his investment was faring. Lenore could still remember glancing down from the stage and seeing Zachary staring up at her. It had been like a scene from the movies. Their eyes had met and Lenore had known, instinctively, that this was the man she wanted to spend the rest of her life with.

Zachary must have been similarly smitten with her, whether he admitted it to himself or not, for he'd made a beeline for her during a break and it was over a polystyrene mug of coffee and a quite intimate little chat—mostly about herself—that she fell even more deeply and hopelessly in love. After Zachary left that day, the memory of him had filled her thoughts and dreams, blocking out even her ambition to be a famous actress. All she wanted was Zachary...

That night, Lenore broke off with her current boyfriend, after which she had settled down to wait impatiently for the handsome solicitor to visit the theatre once more. And it was during this harrowing wait that she'd accidentally found out he was a married man with two young sons.

She'd been devastated. And shocked. And angry. He should have told her, she reasoned irrationally.

When Zachary finally returned to the theatre during the last week of rehearsals, she'd done her best to remain cool and distant, especially when he'd singled her out for his attentions a second time. And she'd managed quite well, yet when he finally left she'd felt utterly wretched, so much so that when rehearsals were over and she realised Zachary hadn't left at all, but had merely retreated into the dark recesses of the theatre to watch, she'd been overcome with a delighted relief.

The upshot was she had stayed chatting with him for far too long and missed her bus home. After a momentary hesitation, Zachary had offered to drive her, which was rather out of his way since she shared a small flat with another girl at Maroubra and he lived somewhere on the North Side of Sydney.

Lenore had known at the time that she should have refused the ride, but wild horses wouldn't have stopped her at that stage. Nevertheless, Zachary hadn't touched her or kissed her or said anything out of line on the way home, but she knew and he knew what was happening between them. The atmosphere in the car had been thick with tension and whenever the car had stopped at a set of lights she'd been hotly aware of his eyes slanting her way, coveting her, wanting her. She'd been more sexually aroused sitting there in that car with just Zachary's eyes on her than she'd been in bed with her boyfriend. Lenore had known, without a doubt, that if and when Zachary ever made love to her she would be transported to the heavens.

But Zachary didn't make love to her. He let her out of the car with a rather curt farewell and accelerated away as though the hounds of hell were after him. And maybe they had been, Lenore recognised. She had certainly reached the state where right and wrong had ceased to have meaning, and the devil himself had been whispering his wicked temptations in her ear.

She hadn't seen Zachary again till the party after the opening night of the play, thrown by Byron at Belleview. Zachary had attended—as he had the play—with his wife, Felicity. He'd studiously avoided Lenore all night, though she did catch him once looking her way, his eyes darkening with undoubted desire when they roved over the admittedly daring little black dress she was almost wearing.

Petticoat in style, it had had tiny shoestring straps holding up a short sheath of satin that slithered over the curves of her tall willowy figure, ending a few meagre inches past her buttocks, exposing a wide expanse of firm creamy thighs. Her hair, which had been even longer then, had completed her highly sensual image by tumbling halfway down her back in a riot of bronzed curls. Outrageous gold earrings had reached from her lobes to her bare shoulders.

Lenore's unrequited love for Zachary—along with several glasses of champagne—had sparked a wild recklessness in her that night, and when she'd seen his lone figure stroll out on to the back patio she couldn't resist following him. One part of her had still been angry with him for having played with her feelings, the rest had been on fire to be with him, no matter what.

But before she'd reached him, he continued down the patio steps, wandering off into the extensive gardens at the side of the house so that by the time Lenore caught up with him they were quite removed from the house and the other partygoers. In fact, they'd moved into the shadows of the trees, and were as alone as they would have been in the most private of bedrooms.

'Zachary!' she called out breathlessly from behind him.

He spun round, his eyes flinging wide with momentary shock before he could successfully gather himself. 'Good God, Lenore, what are you doing out here?' he said with cold anger. 'Go back inside.'

'No,' she panted, her small braless breasts with their erect nipples rising and falling in a ragged, unrehearsed rhythm. 'I won't go back inside and I won't keep pretending. I...I love you, Zachary. You must know that. And I think you love me. D—don't you?'

She was very close to him now, green eyes filled with a very enticing confusion as she gazed up into his face.

'Oh, Zachary, don't torture me so,' she burst out. 'Tell me if you don't love me, for pity's sake.'

'For pity's sake?' His laughter was hard and bitter. 'What do you know of pity, you green-eyed temptress?' And with a sudden groan he swept her against him and kissed her till they were both struggling for breath. He might have drawn back then but Lenore was like a hunting tigress who had finally brought down her prey. She dug her claws in deep and drew him back into her den of desire, her mouth finding his again, her tongue inviting him with an erotic dance that sent a low growl of passion rumbling in his throat.

His mouth never lifted from hers as shaking fingers pushed the straps from her shoulders and the dress concertinaed at her feet. His hands were quite rough as they raked down her arms, and when they reached her thighs they gripped the soft flesh there with something like anger for a second before sliding upwards till they found her aching swollen breasts. She moaned softly as his thumbs rubbed roughly over her nipples, making them harden ever further. Her head was whirling madly, her conscience thoroughly routed, when suddenly, abruptly, he abandoned her.

She could not understand what had happened for a second as she stood there, limbs still trembling, eyes wildly dilated, till Zachary picked up her dress and practically threw it to her. 'No, Lenore,' he said harshly. 'No.'

'But... but you *love* me!'

'Yes, I love you,' he ground out. 'God forgive me, but I do. And perhaps you *think* you love me back. But you'll get over me, Lenore, if I let you. You're only nineteen. You'll soon fall in love with someone else if I have enough courage to turn my back on what you've just offered to me. God, but you're such an innocent, despite your womanly wiles! You've probably been thinking I might divorce Felicity and marry you.'

She clutched her dress in front of her and blinked up at him in disbelief. Surely, if he loved her, he *would* divorce Felicity and marry her! How could he go back to his wife's bed, when it was her—*Lenore*—that he loved and wanted?

'I won't leave my wife and my sons for you,' he announced with a brutal frankness. 'I won't *ever* marry you. Oh, I could set you up somewhere and visit your bed on a regular basis. I could treat you with cool disregard when we run into each other in public, then ravish you behind closed doors. Believe me, I'm sorely tempted to do just that, and if you think you could stop me, then you don't know yourself very well. But eventually you'd grow to hate me as I would grow to hate myself. So let's forget we've ever said these things to each other, let's forget these stolen moments. Grow up, Lenore. Put your dress back on and we'll return to the party, where I'll dance with my wife and you'll dance with our handsome young playwright and we won't mention this incident ever again.'

Lenore had stood there in utter shock when Zachary had done just that. The pain when she'd seen him later in Felicity's arms, smiling into her eyes as though nothing had happened—*nothing*!—had sent a crazed need for vengeance stampeding through her veins. Oh, yes, she'd danced with Nathan all right, danced and drunk champagne, danced and flirted and generally been as irresistibly alluring as an up-and-coming young actress could be when she set her mind to it.

Nathan, in return, had danced her right home into his bed where he'd made love to her with a devastating thoroughness that had stunned and horrified her, for she had found herself responding to his amazingly expert caresses with a quivering pleasure which she'd been sure Zachary alone could evoke. When Nathan's body had finally fused with hers, he'd brought her inexorably to a climax she'd found shattering in more ways than one.

Lenore had woken the next morning, physically sated but mentally confused. Maybe she hadn't loved Zachary after all.

But she *had*!

It wasn't till after she'd been married to Nathan for a while that she learnt to her misery the difference between sex and love. One without the other left her feeling emotionally desolate. It had taken a chance meeting with Zachary soon after Kirsty was born to make her face the empty nature of her relationship with Nathan and make her realise Zachary would always have her heart.

And it had taken *this* chance meeting, today, to ram this fact home one more crushing time.

'Zachary!' she blurted out, determined to say something. Anything!

'Yes?'

'I...I...how's Felicity and the boys?' she finished, hating herself for her lack of courage.

'They're fine. Emery's at university now, in his first year of law. Clark's doing his HSC this year. Would you believe he wants to go into the airforce and become a pilot? I knew I shouldn't have let him watch *Top Gun* a few years back when he was only an impressionable thirteen.'

Lenore noticed he hadn't said anything specific about Felicity and she wasn't about to ask.

An awkward silence descended between them and Lenore was about to say she had to go when Zachary spoke.

'Have you seen the new play at the Royal?'

'*Women at Work*? Yes, I have. It's very good.'

'You wouldn't like to see it again, would you?'

Lenore stared at him.

'Felicity and I had tickets for tonight but she's been called away. Her sister is going through a divorce and breaks down with regular monotony and Felicity feels compelled to dash off and give sisterly succour. She told me to take someone else to the play but really, there was no one I could ask at the last moment, so I wasn't going to bother to go at all, but...'

'I'd love to,' Lenore said quickly, and held her breath.

He gave her a long look which could have meant anything. 'Just as friends, Lenore,' he warned curtly. 'Nothing more.'

'Of course. What shall I wear?'

His smile carried a wealth of self-mockery. 'Sackcloth and ashes?'

She laughed. 'Sackcloth and ashes coming up.'

'And you might leave off that tantalising damned perfume you always used to wear. The thought of sitting next to you in a darkened theatre with *that* on would be more than any man could bear.'

Lenore stared up into his blazing blue eyes and saw the blistering desire hiding behind the harshly delivered humour. Heat zoomed into her cheeks and a quivering started deep within.

Perhaps he saw her arousal, for a very real worry leapt into his face, though it was quickly hidden by a sardonic smile. 'I suppose you wouldn't let me take that invitation back, would you?'

'*Never*,' she said with far too much emotion.

'That's what I thought. Ah, well, perhaps it will have its pluses. There've been quite a few things I've wanted to know over the years, Lenore, my love, things that have eaten into me, things I couldn't very well ask in front of Felicity.'

'What things?'

'They can wait till tonight,' he bit out. 'I must get along to see Byron now.' He actually went to leave her.

'But...but...we haven't made proper arrangements for tonight. Don't you want my address? What time do you want me to be ready by?'

He turned back to face her, his smile bitter. 'My dear Lenore, I have no intention of picking you up at your home. Do I look a fool? I'm already walking a dangerous tightrope taking you to this play at all, a tightrope which you will undoubtedly enjoy rocking at every available opportunity. That's the nature of the beast. He reached out and traced a quivering finger down her cheek and across her mouth, his voice remaining hard but his eyes like the craters of an exploding volcano.

'I have you taped, Lenore. I understand you entirely. After all these years of cold common sense, I'll not play with fire now. It's one thing to sit together at a play, quite another to be alone with you in a car and have to drop you home afterwards.'

Her eyes widened with the understanding of how dangerous he would find that, how dangerous he found being with her except in the most public of places. She grabbed his hand in both of hers and held it. 'You still love me, don't you?' she whispered breathlessly.

Her open accusation startled him, his shock finding solace in a harsh rephrasing. 'I still *want* you. That's hardly the same.'

'You're a liar,' she said, and, opening the palm of his hand, she lifted it to her mouth.

Zachary stared, wide-eyed, as her lips pressed in blind passion to his flesh. Abruptly, he snatched his hand away. 'Stop it, Lenore. Good God, you haven't changed, have you? When are you going to grow up?'

Though shaken by her own actions of a moment ago, she looked him straight in the eye. 'I'm grown up enough to know what the truth is and to say it out loud. You love me and I love you. It can't be wrong to tell the truth, Zachary.'

'It *can* be wrong to tell the truth, Lenore,' he said fiercely. 'It can cause much more pain than lies. Always remember that.' He drew right back then, shaking his head at her with a rueful smile on his face. 'All these years and a moment's weakness could ruin everything. But I don't seem to have the courage to deny myself one miserable evening of your undoubtedly stimulating company. But do try to behave tonight, Lenore,' he warned bitterly. 'Give a man a break. That's all I ask ...'

She nodded in silent acquiescence, totally unable to speak. Zachary loved her. Nothing else mattered.

'I'll meet you in the foyer of the theatre around seven-thirty,' he said. 'The play starts at eight.' And then he was spinning on this heels and striding away down the hospital corridor, not looking back, never looking back.

Lenore stared after him, her heart racing, her head whirling. And then his last words sank in. Behave, he'd said. She'd always had trouble behaving around Zachary. Would tonight be any different?

'Where on earth have you been, Mum?' Kirsty complained when Lenore hurried over to her car, her face flushed.

'I ran into an old friend at the lifts,' she admitted, 'and I simply couldn't get away. I'm sorry. At least you had the foresight to put on the air-conditioning.'

'Oh, that wasn't me, that was Gemma's doing. Not that *she* felt hot. She reckons compared to Lightning Ridge this is cool!'

'It is,' Gemma laughed. 'Anything under forty in the summer is cool.'

'My God, how did you stand it?' Lenore said, having difficulty concentrating on anything but where she would be in three hours' time.

'We didn't wear too many clothes, for starters.'

The mention of clothes reminded Lenore of her mission from Byron regarding Gemma's wardrobe, but it didn't seem the right moment to say anything about that. Nathan was away for the weekend and most of the shops were shut so it could wait till Monday, at least.

'What videos are we going to get?' Kirsty piped up happily.

Lenore frowned. She hated having to back out of their arrangements regarding tonight and hoped Kirsty wouldn't mind. She would stick almost to the truth, though giving the impression that the 'old friend' she'd bumped into was a woman and that she'd been talked into going to the theatre with her tonight.

Kirsty didn't mind at all, which gave Lenore another twinge of jealousy regarding Gemma's growing place in her daughter's life, till she realised she was being silly. Of course Kirsty preferred Gemma's company to her mother's. The girl was more her age!

Thinking of Gemma shifted Lenore's mind back to Nathan and her belief that he was going to seduce that girl. He might not consciously know it yet but it was as inevitable as the sun rising in the east and setting in the west. Gemma's only salvation would be if he got wrapped up in writing another play. Hopefully, he'd finished that play Byron had mentioned a while back, so that he'd be itching to start on another.

Nathan wrote an average of one play a year, the process involving him intensely for up to six months. During this creative period his need for sex was greatly diminished. Hopefully, Nathan was up there at Avoca this weekend, furiously writing away. Creating a new play and having to work at Whitmore Opals at the same time should really tire him out. Still, the last thing he needed was a revamped Gemma swanning around Belleview. Lenore vowed to hold back on her makeover promise for a little while longer, giving Gemma's undoubted virtue a fighting chance. She was far too nice a girl to be wasted on a unfeeling bastard like Nathan.

'Mum!' Kirsty complained with a disgruntled sigh. 'You've just driven straight past the video shop. Truly, you're becoming a real daydreamer when you drive these days.'

'Sorry. My mind was elsewhere, I admit.'

'What on?'

'Oh, nothing important...'

Lenore's stomach was beginning to churn with forbidden excitement by the time she dropped the girls off and headed for home. It was no use. She could tell herself a million times that this was just a platonic date with Zachary but she didn't believe it. Not after what he'd said. She knew that she would sit there beside him in the darkened theatre, fantasising the same things he was fantasising.

Thunder rumbled overhead and Lenore peered up through the windscreen. A summer storm was threatening, white thunderheads mixed with the grey of more ominous-looking clouds. It looked like being an electrical storm, a regular happening after such a hot sultry day.

Lenore wasn't frightened of the storm gathering in the sky, however. It was the storm gathering in her own body that was troubling her. She could feel the tingle of nerve-endings suddenly alert, feel the warm heat of desire igniting the blood in her veins. It had been a long time since she'd experienced the release of sexual satisfaction. Too long, perhaps.

Zachary didn't know the full extent of the danger he was placing himself in tonight. But Lenore was not about to tell him. She didn't appreciate the extent of it herself.

CHAPTER EIGHT

LENORE parked her car in the underground car park beneath the building that housed the Royal Theatre. By seven-twenty on a Saturday night all levels were filling rapidly but she managed to find a spot. She kept repeating the 'yellow' colour-code of the level in the lift afterwards to imprint it on her mind. The last time she'd parked down there, she'd been distracted and forgotten what level she was parked on and it had taken her nearly an hour to find her car.

The lift doors shot open and she joined the passers-by in the curving arcade that went in all directions, one of them to the Theatre Royal. Anyone not knowing where they were heading could easily get lost, she thought, but she'd been to the Royal more times than she could count. She'd even performed there a few times, though only in minor parts.

Most of her acting career had been relegated to minor roles so far. Not because she wasn't a good actress, she believed, but because she didn't curry favour with the right people. Acting was the same as any other showbiz industry. You had to be part of the 'in' crowd to succeed. If you were 'in' you were at the head of the table, given first choice of anything on offer. Everyone else scrambled for the crumbs.

Sleeping with the right people might have helped, she supposed. But that just wasn't her style. Which was ironic, really. She'd slept with Australia's rising star of a playwright for years and it hadn't earned her a single decent role. But that had been deliberate sabotage on Nathan's part, in her opinion. He'd always said she wasn't suited to the women he created, but she knew he'd hated her not being home at night when and if he decided he needed her body.

God, but that man was a selfish chauvinist of the first order! She must enlighten Gemma of his true nature before it was too late.

Lenore gave herself a mental shake, astonished that she could be thinking of anyone other than Zachary at this point in time. But maybe she'd been deliberately diverting her mind from him in an effort to keep her emotions under control tonight. Right from the moment she'd dropped the girls off at Belleview she'd been fighting herself and the inevitable excitement growing within her.

When she'd arrived home, she'd been positively useless for a while, pacing mindlessly through the various rooms, unable to eat, unable even to think about what she would wear. Several times she'd contemplated ringing Zachary and telling him she had changed her mind. It would be the right thing to do.

Lenore knew that she wasn't as strong as Zachary. Normally. But from what she'd witnessed that afternoon, he was going through a stage where he wasn't so strong either. Maybe Felicity was neglecting him sexually. Maybe she was just neglecting him all round. He'd sounded resigned to her going off at all hours to be with her sister. Maybe the marriage was in trouble at long last.

Did Lenore want that? Did she want Zachary to turn to her chiefly because of his wife's neglect? Did she want him in a moment of weakness?

The answers to those questions had obliterated her conscience. Yes, yes, yes! She didn't give a damn what the reason was. She didn't care. All she knew was she wanted Zachary to take her in her arms at least one more time, have him tell her he loved her, hold her, kiss her, touch her. It didn't matter if they didn't go to bed. She was willing to settle for anything, for the crumbs.

Lenore had ground to a halt in front of the large lounge-room window and gazed up at the darkening sky.

I'm wicked, she had told the sky as it spat with lightning and rolled with thunder. I'm just plain wicked.

Yet I don't *feel* wicked, she puzzled now as she hurried across the hard floor of the arcade, her high heels clacking noisily. I feel like a young girl going off on her first date, like a virgin bride on her wedding-night, like a person going to a reunion with their best friend after not seeing them for many, many years.

If only Zachary could have been all of those things, she thought with a lump in her throat. Her first lover, her husband, her best friend . . .

I must not cry, came the swift edict, and she blinked madly. I've spent an hour doing this thirty-four-year-old· face up to look like a rosy innocent young thing and I'm not going to mess it up!

Zachary was there waiting for her, as she'd hoped he would be, looking devastatingly handsome in a black dinner suit. Oh, God, she thought as she walked across the carpeted foyer of the theatre to where he was standing at one end of the bar, two glasses of champagne at the ready.

He watched her come towards him like a starved man, his eyes hungry upon her, his jaw and shoulders squaring in an effort, perhaps, to stop himself from rushing forward. She herself was finding it difficult not to run into his arms, though a sudden jelliness in her thighs would have made running a highly risky mode of movement at that moment. At long last, she was before him, a tremulous smile on her coral-painted mouth.

'Lenore,' he said with superb control, yet his gaze was still drinking in every inch of her slender form, encased that night in a cream suit with gold buttons which revealed nothing and hinted at everything. Her hair was up, tiny Titian tendrils curling around her face and neck. There were pearls in her earlobes and Arpège perfume drenched all over her. She'd remembered what he'd said about *not* wanting to smell her in the darkness of the theatre.

Now she shivered slightly at the thought. It was a shiver of the most sexual kind.

'Zachary,' she returned, and on impulse held out her hand to be kissed.

A wry smile touched Zachary's mouth, a mouth some women might have thought hard and uncompromising. But it was a mouth that had fascinated Lenore for years. Oh, to have that mouth on hers, to have it rove at will over her body...

She watched, dry-mouthed, as he lifted her hand to his lips, swallowing convulsively at the point of contact. She'd always known his lips would be warm, not cold. Soft, not hard.

'Is this an example of you behaving, Lenore?' he mocked as he let go her hand. 'First you arrive looking like the first breath of spring, then you have me kiss you before I've had a chance to recover my equilibrium.'

Green eyes glittering with arousal, Lenore found herself already on that merry-go-round to nowhere which Zachary put her on without any conscious effort. But she could have endured that willingly if it hadn't been for this unexpected shift in manner. His eyes had hardened with that kiss to a brittle blue, his expression becoming cold. Where had the desire-charged Zachary of a few moments ago gone to all of a sudden?

'I seem to remember you like champagne,' he said drily as he handed her a glass and picked the other up for himself.

'Do I?' She frowned for a second before realising what he was referring to. The night of the party at Belleview. A flush of guilt reinforced her already high colour.

'Ah, I see you've remembered the occasion to which I refer. Move over here a little, Lenore.' Taking her elbow, he guided her into a more private corner.

Lenore's thoughts stayed with that most unfair barb of his and she could not remain silent. 'I needed to get drunk that night, Zachary,' she defended shakily. 'Surely you must appreciate that.'

'Did you need to jump into Nathan's bed as well?' he drawled. 'Tell me, Lenore, how do you think I felt when I received the invitation to your wedding less than three months later, when your baby was born nine months to the day from that night?'

Lenore paled. 'You mean you...?'

'Counted back?' He laughed, his mouth lifting in a travesty of a smile. 'Oh, yes, Lenore, I counted, and I found it...*telling*...that the night you told me you loved me you gave yourself to another man. But of course I appreciated in the end that you hadn't really been in love with me. A lot of young women become infatuated with older married men. It's something to do with such men being a challenge.

'The young women in question—who are invariably tantalisingly lovely—like to prove that they're irresistible. One such woman took my father away from my mother, and subsequently from his three children. I, being the eldest, witnessed most of my mother's pain, and ultimately my father's as well. His charming new wife decided after a mere eighteen months that he was, after all, too old for her. She left a trail of destruction behind, I can tell you.'

Lenore wasn't sure if she felt sorry for Zachary, or furious with him. She was sympathetic with the hell he'd gone through as a child, and she understood now why he was so strong on sticking with his marriage through thick and thin. But if he was placing her on a par with the woman who had destroyed his parents' marriage, if he thought her shallow and cruel...

'I was *not* one of those young women,' she insisted fiercely.

'Weren't you? Can you say that if I left my wife for you you wouldn't have grown tired of me after a while, that you wouldn't have felt the need eventually to flex your feminine power on some other unsuspecting male?'

Lenore's anger flared even further. 'You were never unsuspecting, Zachary. You sought *me* out in the beginning, not the other way around.'

A guilty colour slashed across his high cheekbones. 'I couldn't seem to keep away,' he muttered.

'Then blame yourself,' she snapped. 'Not me.'

They glared at each other.

Suddenly, the hardness around Zachary's mouth softened to a sardonic smile. 'You are so right, Lenore. So very right. It *was* my fault in the beginning. I knew you were forbidden fruit. I watched you on that stage, so beautiful and clever and fiery. And I told myself I only wanted to talk to you, that I could control what I was feeling. I played with fire and I got burnt.'

'I . . . I got burnt too, Zachary,' she choked out.

'Did you, Lenore? Or were you just scorched a little? I think perhaps I ignited you just enough for some other man to come along and quench your fire. That's what kills me the most, to think it was *my* fault you went to bed with Nathan. My God,' he groaned. 'I virtually pushed you at him.'

'Stop it, Zachary,' Lenore hissed. 'Just stop it! Blaming ourselves or each other for what happened is futile. What happened happened. But be assured I never loved Nathan. I slept with him, I married him, I had a child by him. But I never loved him. I divorced him, god-dammit, because I couldn't stand another night of lying in his bed and wishing it were you beside me!'

Zachary's face grew ashen as he stared at her. He uttered a brief obscenity then swept the champagne glass to his lips, gulping deeply. His hand was shaking and his eyes, when they lifted, looked bruised and haunted.

Lenore felt dreadful. Why, oh, why hadn't she kept her stupid mouth shut? Zachary had enough to bear without her burdening him with her own self-inflicted miseries. But at least he now knew she'd genuinely loved him. He hadn't been some passing fancy. For him to have kept on believing that was the case would have been intolerable!

They kept staring at each other in the most ghastly silence, and Lenore accepted that once again their love for each other was proving to be a highly destructive force.

Its chemistry sizzled across the space between them, tormenting and tantalising, making them dissatisfied with their present existences, making them want what they shouldn't want. Both of them knew that to give in to their desires would ultimately render them wretched with guilt.

The buzzer announcing that it was time to be seated splintered the appalling atmosphere just in time. Zachary took the glass from Lenore's hands with a tight little smile and placed it with his on the bar before returning to take her elbow.

'Let's try and enjoy the play, shall we?' he said tautly. 'I expect it might be the last thing either of us enjoys for quite some time.'

Zachary behaved impeccably over the next three hours, not touching Lenore in the darkened theatre, not whispering anything suggestive in her ear, not putting a foot out of place. He played the role of platonic friend to perfection, making trite conversation when required, escorting her to the foyer at intermission where he secured her another glass of champagne before taking her back inside to see the second half of what was probably a riveting performance, if Lenore had been in the mood to be riveted.

She could not remember a single moment of either half, but she had seen the play before so could make suitable comments at suitable moments, such as when the curtain finally fell.

'It truly is a wonderful play,' she sighed.

'If you say so.'

Her sideways glance revealed a face like stone. The play was over and so was the night. He looked as grim as she felt.

'Where are you parked?' he asked as they made slow progress out of the theatre. The session had been packed.

'Underneath. Level Yellow.'

'I'm on Blue. I'll walk you to your car. I don't like these car parks much. Ideal places for women to be raped.'

'Really?' Lenore couldn't help it. She raised her eyebrows in black humour at Zachary, who tried to look reproachful but failed.

A rueful smile smoothed the frown from his forehead. 'If I did, you'd scream bloody murder.'

'Probably,' she laughed softly.

His eyes dropped briefly to her parted lips before he reefed them away, that steely mask clanging back into place.

Lenore sighed.

Several people exited from the lift on Level Yellow so that they were not strictly alone as Zachary walked her to her car. It seemed a very short walk to Lenore, she imagined as short as the walk from a murderer's cell down the corridor of death to the electric chair. Leaving Zachary's company was as horrifying a prospect as dying. In fact it *was* a little like dying.

Fumbling in her gold evening bag, she extracted her car keys and was just fitting them into the lock of the driver's door when she noticed the front right-hand tyre. It was as flat as a tack.

'Oh, no,' she groaned. 'Look at that.'

Zachary looked, and shrugged. 'It happens. I presume you have a spare? I'll change it for you.'

'Yes,' she said, a ghastly curl of guilt fluttering in her stomach as she recalled something. 'But...I—er—it's flat too.'

Zachary gave her a sharp, narrow-eyed glare.

'I...meant to get it fixed...'

'And how long has it been flat?' he asked curtly.

'Ages, I'm afraid. I—er—keep forgetting. Besides, I didn't think I could possibly have two flat tyres in the one year. Before that I'd never had *one*!'

Lenore knew she sounded irresponsible, which was not like her at all, but in matters relating to cars she'd been more than happy for Nathan to take charge. Since the divorce, she'd been letting things slide where her car was concerned and she really would have to get her act together.

'I'm sorry, Zachary...'

'Are you? I doubt that, Lenore. I doubt that very much. I'll have to drive you home now, I suppose.'

'I could take a taxi...'

'So you could. Is that what you want to do?'

'No.'

'I didn't think so. Come along, then. We'll pick up the spare tyre as we drive past, drop it in at a garage on the way home and come back to pick up your car tomorrow morning.'

'Tomorrow? But...but...'

'Felicity won't be returning till tomorrow evening. We're in no danger of being caught, if that's what you're afraid of.'

Something in Zachary's tone sparked a flash of anger in Lenore. 'We're not doing anything really *wrong*!' she insisted.

Zachary laughed. The laugh was bad enough, but the wild glitter in his eyes unnerved Lenore completely. Was he in danger of going over some indefinable edge?

'Let's go, Lenore,' he said brusquely, and grabbed her upper arm.

He practically dragged her over to the lift, displaying a side of his nature she'd never encountered before. Or had she? He'd been a pretty tough character the night of that party.

'Hey! Cut out the rough stuff,' she complained as he shoved her into the thankfully empty lift. 'I happen to bruise easily.'

Savage blue eyes lanced the fair, faintly freckled skin of her bare arm which was already showing fingermarks on the softer underside. 'How inconvenient for you,' he drawled, 'especially in the summer.'

'Meaning?'

'Meaning you must own some good body make-up, since I've never seen any marks on you. Or was Nathan an exceptionally tender lover? Somehow, I can't imagine you liking tenderness, Lenore. You're far too tempestuous by nature.'

She crossed her arms and fell sulkily silent. She didn't like Zachary in this mood. It wasn't *her* fault the tyre had been flat. Yet he was clearly furious at having to spend more time with her. Did he think she had planned it? That this was some devious ploy to get him to take her home?

Yes, of course that was what he thought!

She grabbed the sleeve of his dinner-jacket. 'I didn't plan this, Zachary. You must believe me!'

His sidewards glance was cold. 'Just leave it for now, Lenore.'

'No, I—'

'Leave it!' he spat out.

She left it.

Zachary's dark maroon Jaguar was a sheer delight to ride in but Lenore was beyond noticing, or caring. They swept in wretched silence up the ramp of the car park and into the night, only to find a southerly squall had blown in after the electrical storm, heavy rain lashing the wind-screen and making driving hazardous. It took all of Zachary's concentration to negotiate the still busy city streets and get them safely over the Harbour Bridge and on to the Pacific Highway, heading for home.

A brief stopover to drop the tyre at a garage on the way brought Zachary back behind the driving wheel with water-spattered shoulders and damp hair. Lenore automatically glanced at him, her heart yearning for him to look back at her with some warmth, but he jerked his face away with a shudder and turned the key in the ignition.

Lenore fell into the deepest depression. He hated her. He despised her. He thought her manipulative and scheming and evil.

It wasn't till Zachary turned down a side-street and slid the car into the kerb right outside her villa home in Tur-ramurra—without any directions from her—that Lenore snapped back to reality.

'How did you know where I lived?' she asked.

'Don't ask,' was his succinct reply.

'But I want to know.'

'Shut up, Lenore. Shut up and get out of this car.'

Oddly enough, he was already climbing out himself, which made nonsense of his attitude towards her. What was going on here?

'Lock the passenger door,' he ordered testily. 'I don't want to come out here tomorrow morning and find the damned thing stolen.'

She locked the door before his words sank in. Suddenly, her eyes snapped up, wide with shock and bewilderment.

'I can fight myself, Lenore,' he said with a raw, bitter passion. 'I can even fight you. But I can't fight fate. Yes, I'm going to spend the night with you. And if you say one word of protest, if you find one single solitary excuse why I can't, I swear to God I won't be responsible for the consequences!'

CHAPTER NINE

LENORE felt the blood begin to drain from her face. But she wasn't, and never had been, a fainting sort of female. So she pulled herself together and walked, with her whirling head held high, up the paved pathway that led round to the side-entrance of her quite luxurious and beautifully furnished two-bedroom town house.

Zachary followed.

She didn't look at him as she unlocked the door and stepped inside, keeping her eyes averted as Zachary brushed past her to stride ahead across the small entry hall and through the archway that led straight into the living-room. Although the room was in darkness, he found, as though by instinct, the lamps on the side-tables at each end of the sofa, switching them on to flood the room with their soft apricot light.

Lenore trailed after him to remain just inside the room to the right of the archway, watching with horrified fascination as Zachary discarded his bow-tie, stripped off his jacket, then started on the buttons of his white dress shirt.

'What...what do you think you're doing?'

His eyes mocked her from beneath their dark brows. 'I'm getting undressed, Lenore. I would have thought that was pretty obvious. Please don't be coy. I won't like you coy.'

A choked sound flew from her throat. 'I don't think you like me at all! Why must you reduce what we feel for each other to this?' she cried. 'It...it's disgusting. I won't have it, do you hear?'

'You won't have it?' He laughed and with a few appallingly quick strides grabbed her stunned body by the upper arms and drove her back against the wall. 'You'll have it any way I choose to give it to you,' he threatened. 'And you'll love it!'

She gaped into his passion-dark face and felt afraid of him for the first time in her life. Her fear must have been mirrored in her eyes for suddenly he groaned and drew her shocked body to his, cradling her head against his shoulder, and doing his best to stop the uncontrollable tremors that were racking her slender frame.

'I'm sorry,' he rasped. 'I didn't mean that. Dear God, I didn't mean it.'

Lenore finally began to cry, sobs tearing from her chest with dry, gasping sounds.

'I...I love you,' she blurted out. 'You must...believe me.'

'Yes, yes,' he crooned, and continued to soothe her while pulling the pins from her hair, stroking the gold-red waves down her back till her sobs were reduced to the occasional whimper and she was clinging to him.

'Yes,' he said at last with a return to steely resolve, and stepped back to rapidly undo the buttons of her jacket and drag it down off her shoulders till it fell into a crumpled heap in the carpet.

Her bra was nothing but a wisp of cream lace and satin designed to allure rather than support, for her small, firm breasts required no such foundation. Naked, they stood high and beautifully shaped, their long pink nipples invitingly tipped up as though soliciting a man's mouth.

When Zachary removed her bra he groaned and bent his lips to do their silent bidding.

Lenore gasped, her heart racing behind the breast he was so deliciously savouring. 'Oh, God,' she cried when his fingers started plucking at her other nipple at the same time, her desire flaring out of control.

She braced her palms against the wall beside her lest her knees give way entirely, giving herself up to Zachary's will with a blind, impassioned need that years of denial had created. The man she loved was finally making love to her and it was everything she envisaged. And more.

It was wild.

His mouth moved across to that other breast, sucking furiously now, his hand dropping to the waistband of her skirt, and soon it too joined the jacket and bra on the floor. Now only her panties, tights and shoes prevented her from being totally naked before him, and already the first two were being peeled down her body.

He gasped away from her breast to hurriedly complete the stripping away of her clothes, leaving her panting and nude against the wall. When he had scooped all her clothes out of their way, he straightened to stare at her, hot eyes feasting on her body for several arousing moments before lifting to meet her own wide, desire-filled gaze.

'I've thought about this moment for so long,' he said hoarsely. 'I've pictured it in my mind, imagined what I would do, how I would feel. But the reality is so different from my fantasies. I should have known... Hell, I should have known...'

His eyes held her in thrall as he ripped his shirt aside then proceeded to discard the rest of his clothes, never once letting his hypnotic gaze move from hers. And when he too was naked, he pressed his aroused body against hers, taking her hands in his, entwining their fingers and lifting them high above her head, squeezing tightly while he took her mouth in a kiss that was deceptively tender at first. But it built and built in power and passion till they were both beside themselves with longing to be one.

There was no question of going elsewhere, of finding some soft bed for their first union. Their need for each other was too strong and immediate for any further delay. Was it her own shaking hands that guided him inside, or was it his around hers? Lenore wasn't sure. She only knew she cried out as she felt his flesh fill hers and everything began to swirl in a black haze within her head. She felt hot and breathless and her hands were now miraculously gripping his shoulders and he was driving up into her with an impassioned rhythm that gave no thought to anything but achieving nature's objective.

Lenore was catapulted to a climax with amazing speed, her pleasure propelling Zachary into an equally tumultuous release, stunning Lenore with the sheer number of his shuddering gasps, and the length of time it took for his body to rest quietly within her. She'd never experienced anything like it.

'Oh, Zachary…darling…' she whispered when at last his head lifted and he started smoothing her damp hair back from her face.

'I know,' he groaned. 'I know…'

She laid her head on his chest and wrapped her arms tightly around him. 'Just hold me, Zachary. Hold me and never let me go.'

They were embracing each other in a state of mutual bliss when she felt his chest lift in a startled gasp. 'Dear God!' he exclaimed, very much shaken. 'You can't get pregnant, can you? I just didn't think.' His hands lifted to rake back his tousled hair in deep agitation. 'Hell, what have I done? I'm a bloody fool!'

She lifted a gentle hand to lay against his cheek, her smile rueful. 'No need to worry, dearest. Do you think I would let such a thing happen to me twice?'

He frowned down at her. 'You mean you came to the play tonight, prepared for this eventuality? Dear lord, yes, of course you did. Now I'm being naïve.'

A decided chill ran through Lenore. 'No,' she denied. 'I did not come prepared. I happen to be on the Pill. I have been ever since shortly after Kirsty was born. I kept taking it after the divorce because it gave me mental peace.'

'You've had other lovers since the divorce, I suppose,' he muttered.

'No!' she denied again, more forcefully this time. 'I have not. And I don't think of you as a lover, Zachary. You're my love, my one and only love.'

There was reproach in her voice and hurt in her eyes. Zachary said nothing for a moment and when Lenore went to walk away from him he grabbed her and spun her back against him. 'I believe you,' he rasped. 'I must. Oh, my lovely Lenore, my beautiful, irresistible Lenore...' His hands were roving over her once more and she was powerless to stop their excitement. 'Don't let's argue. I want to make love to you all night. I want to put a lifetime of pleasure into a few hours. I want to do everything with you I've always wanted to do...'

Lenore groaned with a type of dismay when he swept her up into his arms and made for the bedroom. Logic demanded Zachary's words held no promise of a future together. But her love for him weakened any resolve to make an issue of his lack of commitment. She also pushed aside the worry that his feelings for her might be nothing but a sexual thing, easily burnt out now that he'd crossed the line which had kept them apart these many years.

But these doubts were quickly forgotten when she was in his arms once more. He must love her to want her so much, she reasoned. He must!

They lay in bed shortly after dawn, watching the rain beat against the window. The curtains were pulled back, their view that of an enclosed and very private courtyard, full of palms and other greenery.

'Did you know Turramurra has the highest rainfall of any suburb in Sydney?' Zachary remarked softly.

'Yes, I had heard that somewhere. It's good for the garden, though.' Lenore sighed the sigh of a sated woman, her body exhausted. She might have drifted off to sleep at long last if that same body hadn't felt the call of nature. 'I have to go to the bathroom,' she said. 'I'll probably have a shower while I'm there. *Alone*, this time,' she threw back over her shoulder.

He laughed and she pulled a face at him. But when she finally made it under the hot jets of water, she found herself recalling Zachary's insistence on having a shower with her earlier in the night, followed by his insistence on several other activities while in there. It really worried

Lenore that this last night had been reduced to nothing more than a fulfillment of all Zachary's fantasies where she was concerned.

Lenore was fully awake by the time she snapped off the shower and dried herself, blowdrying her hair till it fluffed out down her back in a riot of waves. Inspecting her face in the mirror, she found her skin glowing, her eyes bright and her mouth a deep purple. Bruised, most likely, she decided.

She groaned when she looked at the rest of her body. Thank the lord it was raining. It would be long sleeves for her today. Wrapping a towel around herself sarong-style, Lenore left the bathroom and told Zachary that she was hungry and she might as well make some breakfast for them both, so what did he want?

He yawned and stretched, bringing her eyes to the rippling muscles in his broad chest and lean hard stomach. For a man of forty-five he still had an incredible body. 'You mean you're going to feed me as well?' he drawled.

'As well as what?' she retorted.

He totally ignored her, his eyes narrowing with that now familiar look as it raked over her. 'Take off that towel,' he said thickly.

'No. I'm making breakfast.'

'Then make it in the nude. I want you naked, Lenore.'

'Well, if that's all you want then I want you out of here!' she lashed back with such unexpected venom she shocked them both.

But reality had suddenly crashed through Lenore and she hadn't liked what she'd seen, either in Zachary or herself. All those encounters, those positions, those torrid matings. They'd been nothing but sex, she realised with dawning horror.

Oh, she'd deluded herself by calling them love, but they didn't feel like love at this moment. They felt like lust. All of a sudden, she felt cheap and sordid and far, far worse than she had ever felt with Nathan. At least he'd been her husband. *This* man . . . why, he didn't love her either. Not the sort of love she craved. She could see that now.

'You don't mean that,' he rasped, clearly shocked.

'I most certainly do. Go back to your wife, Zachary. I don't want you any more. I . . . I . . .' Her voice broke, as did her heart. Sobbing, she turned to drop her head into shaking hands and cry tears of utter despair.

He was beside her in an instant, taking her in his arms, saying and doing anything to soothe her. But she would not be soothed.

'You don't l . . . love me,' she wailed. 'You just wanted to . . . to . . .'

'No,' he groaned. 'No!' he repeated in a pained shout, shaking her a little. 'That's not true. Maybe I was trying to exorcise you at first, when I took you up against the wall. But you'd sent me crazy with desire over the years, Lenore, whether you meant to or not. Then last night, when your tyre was flat, I couldn't believe that was an accident. I thought . . . the bitch has played me for a sucker. Old tapes went off in my mind and I thought you'd decided to win me through fair means or foul and yes, I lost my temper. Brother, I was so infuriated with you I thought I would explode. But my anger was simply another face of my love for you, just as my lust is another face of my love for you. I wallowed in both last night, Lenore, because they're far safer emotions than love. They can be controlled or superficially satisfied. Love can't. Love goes on and on and on and nothing can ever fill the empty place in my heart that yearns for you and you alone.'

'But you can have me, Zachary,' she burst forth. 'You can get a divorce. *Marry* me.'

'I can't.'

She stared at him. 'You mean you *won't*.'

'That's right,' he said firmly. 'I mean I won't.'

Lenore knew there was no point in arguing with him. His mind was made up. He was the same inflexible Zachary he'd always been, the same stubborn, proud, noble, decent man she'd fallen in love with.

'I see,' she said.

Shrugging his hands from her shoulders, she walked away, both to put a physical distance between them and to give her the opportunity to gather herself for what she was about to say. Finally, she turned, only to find that it might have been better to have remained where she was. To see him standing there in all his naked glory, clearly wanting her again, was hard on her resolve.

Swallowing, she embarked on the most important speech she had ever made in all her life. For she was fighting for her love, fighting for her future and her happiness. 'Yes, I really do see, Zachary. You have a code of standards or beliefs which demand that your marriage must be saved regardless of your feelings or mine. Your first loyalty—and priority—is to your wife and children. A very laudable commitment, and one which I appreciate and understand, especially now that you've told me about what happened with your parents.

'I admire you for your stance, Zachary. I always have. In the past, I would have said you did the right thing. Without question. But now...today...I believe you might be making a mistake to keep on throwing yourself on the sacrificial pyre of a marriage that can't possibly be making you happy. Your boys are nearly men. Your wife seems more interested in her sister's welfare than yours. Don't your own feelings rate here? Or mine?'

'No,' he said sternly. 'They don't. I made a vow, Lenore. I mean to keep that vow.'

'You broke it last night,' she pointed out, more in desperation than a desire to hurt him. But he looked pained all the same.

'That's my guilt to carry around. But Felicity will never know if we never tell her. Our marriage can go on as before.'

'You honestly believe that?'

'I do. As I said to you once, the truth can hurt, far more than lies. I would only hurt her by confessing our affair. I'd certainly hurt her if I divorced her. You don't know Felicity, Lenore. She's a sweet, gentle soul who needs a man to look after her. Oh, I admit she wasn't the right match for me all along, but I didn't know that till after she was pregnant with Emery and then it was too late. But she's been a good wife, and she's a damned good mother to my sons. I can't find happiness over her misery, Lenore. And I won't destroy my sons' good opinion of me.'

'But how can you go from my bed back to hers?' Lenore wailed.

'But you'll do it?' she gasped.

'Yes.'

'My God...'

'I could stand it, Lenore, if I knew I could see you from time to time.'

When he came towards her, she backed away in horror. 'No, don't you touch me. Don't you touch me ever again.' Tears began streaming down her face, tears of frustration and desolation. 'I...I want you to go. And I don't want you ever to come back.'

His face was grim, his eyes hollow and haunted. 'You would condemn me to that, Lenore? I thought you loved me...'

It was too much. His face. His words. The emptiness in his voice. With a cry of torment Lenore threw herself, weeping, back into his arms.

CHAPTER TEN

'How intriguing, Gemma,' Ava said as she stared at the old photograph, then at Gemma's birth certificate. 'What do you think, Melanie?'

'I think Gemma's assumption about her real age is probably correct,' was Melanie's considered opinion. 'But there *is* a slim possibility this is your mother pregnant with a child before *you*, Gemma, a child that might not have lived.'

Gemma frowned at this possibility, which had never occurred to her. It was a logical thought, yet everything inside her rejected it. She was convinced she was older than her birth certificate stated. This was *herself* her mother was pregnant with, not a dead brother or sister. She was sure of it.

'And I suppose there is also a slim possibility that your mother is still alive,' Melanie went on matter-of-factly, 'but I wouldn't like you to get your hopes up. On top of that, this birth certificate could be a complete forgery, full of all sorts of lies.'

Dismay filled Gemma as she picked up the document again and stared at it more closely. A forgery. Her heart sank even further.

'It would also be foolish to presume your parents were married at all. You said you didn't find any marriage certificate in your father's papers.'

'Do you have to keep saying horrible things?' Kirsty burst out crossly. 'Can't you see you're making Gemma unhappy?'

'No, no, Kirsty,' Gemma refuted. 'I wanted to talk about this. I appreciate hearing Melanie's thoughts. It's better I have realistic expectations rather than go round with my head in the clouds.'

'I can't imagine anyone less likely to have her head in the clouds than you, Gemma. What's this all about?'

All four female faces jerked round and up to stare at their unexpected intruder. They'd thought they were alone in the house that Sunday morning. Heavy rain had kept them indoors so they'd decided on a game of Monopoly on the living-room floor, and it was while playing that Ava had started questioning Gemma about her life in Lightning Ridge and soon Gemma had been telling her new friends about the mystery of her birth and her mother. The game had been temporarily abandoned while Gemma produced the photo and her birth certificate for the others to look at and comment on. Now it looked like she would have to show them to a fourth person. Nathan Whitmore.

'Dad!' Kirsty exclaimed with delight on her face. 'What are you doing here?'

'It's not much fun at the beach, sweetie, when it's raining cats and dogs.'

'Oh, *Dad*,' his daughter said with laughter and reproach in her voice. 'As if you ever go down to the beach much anyway. One quick dip and you're back, sitting at that computer of yours, creating away like someone possessed. You should see him, Gemma. Totally off in another world. I could go in and confess to murder and he'd say, "That's nice, sweetie".'

Ava laughed. 'That does sound like you, Nathan, you must admit.'

Melanie climbed gracefully to her feet. 'I'll make you some coffee and a sandwich, Nathan.'

'Thanks, Melanie. I could do with something to eat.'

'That's another thing he forgets to do when he writes, Gemma. Eat! He used to drive Mum up the wall once he got his nose into a new play. So how's it going, Dad? Another ripper for Hollywood to buy like the last one?'

'The only thing ripper about the play I'm working on at the moment,' he countered drily, 'is the amount of paper I'm ripping up. I don't know what's wrong with me. I can't seem to concentrate.'

He came forward, his eyes returning to Gemma who had once again failed miserably not to stare at him. But Nathan in tight blue jeans and a navy blue sweatshirt looked less formidable yet more devastatingly attractive than ever. He sat down in a nearby armchair and leant forward to pick up both the old photograph and the birth certificate which had been dropped back in to the middle of the Monopoly board.

'Has Gemma told you about her mysterious history, Nathan?' Ava asked as his eyes went from the certificate to the photo to the certificate again.

Steely grey eyes lifted to lock with Gemma's nervous brown ones. 'No,' he said. 'She also seems to have made a small miscalculation about her age. According to this...' he waved the birth certificate '...she's only eighteen.'

'That's probably a forgery,' Kirsty piped up before Gemma could fashion her own defence. 'If you turn that photo over, Dad, you'll see it's dated Christmas, 1973. Gemma believes that's her mother pregnant with her so that means she was born early in 1974 which makes her nearly twenty.'

Nathan stared at Gemma, then down at the photo for an elongated time, then up at Gemma once again. 'What do you mean, you *believe* this is your mother? Don't you *know*?'

She shook her head. 'My father refused to speak of her other than to tell me she died when I was born and to say I took after her, though whether he meant in looks or something else I'm not sure. After he died, I found this photograph hidden in his things. It *has* to be my mother. She has the same name. Who else could it be?'

'Who else indeed? Stefan and Mary...' He frowned and glanced at the birth certificate again. 'It says here your father's name is Jon, yet the photo says Stefan. Which one's right, Stefan or Jon?'

'Stefan, I think. He was definitely Swedish. I think the Jon is an alias. As far as the Smith part is concerned . . . it's likely that's an alias as well.'

'Mmm.' Nathan studied the photograph again. 'You seem to have similar colouring to your mother, and a similar shaped face, but it's hard to compare you properly with her wearing sunglasses. You don't seem to take after your father at all, except perhaps in your build. You're a much bigger girl than your mother.'

Gemma flushed when Nathan's eyes flicked to her full breasts which lay braless beneath her thin white top. Thinking he'd be absent from the house that day, she'd dressed very informally in jeans and an old T-shirt. Quite frankly, her bras were of a very cheap variety and they didn't fit all that well. She left them off whenever she could but in truth her breasts were the kind that needed some restraint. Left free, they jiggled alarmingly when she walked. Even when she sat as breathlessly still as she was sitting at that moment, they were an eyeful.

Nathan seemed to have difficulty dragging *his* eyes away from them, a fact which had the most embarrassing effect. Gemma knew if she looked down she would find her nipples poking at the thin material. The sensation was so alien to her—and so shameful—that she desperately wanted to cover herself with her hands. But how could she do that without looking ridiculous? All she could think of was to draw her knees up and lean forward to wrap her arms around them so that her breasts were hidden against her thighs.

Melanie's re-entrance with a small tray of food was a very welcome distraction. 'I see Gemma has shown you the photo and her birth certificate,' the housekeeper said as she placed the tray down on the small table beside the armchair. 'Perhaps you could make some enquiries about her mother for her, Nathan. She's anxious to find out if the lady might be still alive, or, barring that, if some of her family are.'

'Do you want me to do that, Gemma?'

Now she was forced to look back up at him again. 'Yes, I do, but...won't that cost a lot of money?'

'Only if you hire a private investigator. But I don't think that's necessary to begin with. I could get Moira to pop down to the births, deaths and marriages department during her lunch hour. And I have an acquaintance in the police department who could give me some pertinent information. But what makes you think your mother might be still alive? Do you have reason to believe your father lied to you about that?'

'I think my father lied to me about a lot of things,' she murmured, and dropped her eyes again.

'I suppose you're referring to the black opal,' Nathan said on a rueful note.

'What black opal?' Kirsty asked.

'Yes, what black opal, Gemma?' Ava joined in.

She told them about the opal.

'Good grief, Nathan,' Ava burst out after Gemma finished her tale. 'That has to be the opal that disappeared the day Byron married Irene!'

'Yes,' he admitted. 'The Heart of Fire.'

'What a passionate name for a mere opal,' Melanie remarked in her passionless voice. She hadn't rejoined them on the floor, having perched herself instead on the arm of an empty lounge-chair. 'To be honest, I've always thought opals rather cold-looking stones.'

'Not this one,' Nathan said.

'No, certainly not,' Gemma insisted warmly. 'It's the most beautiful thing I've ever seen.'

'I'll bet you were spitting chips when you found out it wasn't yours, Gemma,' Kirsty sympathised. 'I know I would have been.'

Gemma smiled. 'I wasn't too happy. But Byron's given me a lovely reward for bringing it back safe and sound.'

'But how did your father get his hands on the opal?' Ava re-entered the conversation, frowning. 'We always thought it had to have been stolen by one of the guests at the wedding. Or possibly one of the hired helps. Byron was planning to present it to Irene as a gift at the recep-

tion,' she told her intrigued audience. 'The opal was to
be a token gesture to symbolise the healing of the rift between our two families. From what I can vaguely recall,
the opal had something to do with the original feud between Byron's and my father and Irene's father, but I
never did know what, exactly. Do you know what actually happened, Nathan?'

'No, I don't.'

'Well, I suppose it isn't too hard to guess,' Ava swept
on excitedly, clearly in her element. 'I do know David
Whitmore and Stewart Campbell were prospecting partners and best friends once, before they fell out, that is. It
seems reasonable to presume their argument was probably over the opal. Maybe my father found it and refused
to share it with Stewart Campbell.'

She heaved a melodramatic sigh. 'Whatever, they went
their separate ways and became rivals in business, setting up opposing opal-trading companies here in Sydney,
though Campbell's eventually branched out into other
jewellery as well. Even when the original enemies passed
away, their children were left a legacy of hatred and bitterness, especially on the Campbell side, which Byron has
always claimed he hoped to heal by his marriage to Irene.
But I still think—well, I find it hard to believe that—I
mean . . . um—er . . .'

Her voice trailed away and Kirsty immediately jumped
in. 'Don't stop there, Ava! We're all dying of curiosity.
Dad, why haven't you told me any of this fascinating
stuff before? Gosh, it's just like Romeo and Juliet!'

Ava slid worried eyes in the direction of Nathan, who
looked resigned. 'You might as well complete the saga
now, Ava. I won't tell Byron, but don't paint him too
blackly. I'm sure he meant well, and there wasn't a man
in the world who could have made Irene happy.'

'Byron always means well,' Ava muttered. 'Still . . . I
dare say he suffered enough for his greed. Everyone knew
Byron asked Irene to marry him, not because he loved
her, but because he wanted the two companies to merge.
Campbell's marketing strategies with their new chain-

type stores had been putting a big dent in Whitmore Opals' profits for quite a few years. We couldn't compete, especially when Campbell's kept targeting opals as the one gemstone they sold cheaply.

'Unfortunately for Byron, he didn't find out till after the wedding that Campbell's would never belong to Irene. She'd merely let him think that. In reality, when Stewart Campbell died the previous year, control had passed to his second wife, who was not fond of her husband's first-born daughter. Irene's mother had died when she was a baby and her father had quickly married again, a wealthy socialite named Adele who had two children by him—a daughter, Celeste, and a son, Damian. Adele eventually handed over control of Campbell's to her daughter, Celeste, who's proved to be one of the toughest, meanest, cleverest business-women ever to draw breath.'

'Beautiful, though,' Nathan inserted.

'Yes, but bad through and through. She has two pleasures in life, it seems. Scoring victories over Whitmore Opals and sleeping with younger and younger men as she gets older and older.'

'I don't think the young men mind, Ava,' Nathan chuckled drily. 'Would that all women looked as good as Celeste Campbell! Besides, she's not that old. I doubt she's even turned forty yet.'

Gemma told herself it wasn't jealousy that made her direct the conversation to other matters than this detestable-sounding woman whom Nathan felt compelled to compliment. 'But what happened back at Byron's wedding, Ava?' she asked abruptly. 'I want to know how the opal was stolen and what happened afterwards.'

'Didn't I tell you that? I didn't? Sorry.' She smiled. 'I get muddled sometimes. Well, I was a flower-girl at the wedding, and no one told me anything but when you're a little kid in a mostly grown-up household you learn to keep your ears and eyes open. The reception, for some reason, was being held at Belleview—I think the second Mrs Campbell refused to have it at Campbell Court.

'Anyway, if I recall rightly, Byron went into the library just before the sit-down part of the meal started and the wall safe was wide open and the opal gone. Boy, was there a to-do. The police were called and people were searched but the opal was never found. It totally spoilt the reception. People say it was the opal that caused the marriage to go sour, that it brought bad luck, which is hog-wash. Even if Byron had adored Irene and kissed her feet every day, that woman would never have been happy. She was totally—

'Oh, my goodness, Gemma!' Ava broke off abruptly from what she'd been saying. 'An astounding thought has just occurred to me. Maybe your father was an international jewel-thief who came here from Europe and somehow wangled an invitation to the wedding, stole the opal, then spent the rest of his life hiding out at Lightning Ridge so that Interpol couldn't find him.'

'For pity's sake, spare us your romantic solutions, Ava,' Nathan reprimanded impatiently. 'If Gemma's father had been an international jewel-thief, he'd have sold the damned thing to a fence and provided a better life for his daughter than the back-blocks of Lightning Ridge. I doubt very much if he had anything to do with the original theft. Personally, I think he came across the opal quite accidentally and was too afraid to sell it or even show it to anyone. He knew it had to be stolen property.'

'That's as much supposition as what I said,' Ava argued, though feebly.

'Maybe,' he admitted, 'but since the original theft happened so long ago, it would be almost impossible to uncover the truth now one way or the other. Besides, Byron doesn't want it all dragged up again. It would only open old wounds between the Whitmores and the Campbells, and Celeste Campbell has enough knives ready for our backs already.'

Nathan returned to eating his snack and Ava subsided into chastened silence. Gemma felt sorry for her. She was such a dear, but did lack self-confidence. She allowed people to ride roughshod over her far too much. Her barb about Byron always meaning well was very telling, however. Still, maybe she had herself to blame if she allowed others to interfere in her life. She was thirty years old and should not be living in her brother's home off her brother's charity. What she needed was a job and a life of her own!

Thinking of jobs reminded Gemma of her own employment at Whitmore Opals. She was to begin Japanese lessons at a local business college in the morning, attending lectures every Monday, Wednesday and Friday for the next four weeks after which she was supposed to be able at least to make herself understood by a Japanese client. She hadn't said so to Nathan but she found the prospect daunting. If only she'd taken a language at school. But her father had steered her away from what he'd considered high-falutin' subjects.

'I'll keep this birth certificate with me,' Nathan said on finishing his sandwich and coffee. He handed her back the photo. 'Don't expect miracles,' he warned.

'I'm grateful for anything you can find out,' she said with sincerity, meeting his eyes now with far more ease. She'd grown used to his presence and thought her breasts were back to normal. Not that she was risking anything. Her knees would remain up till he left the room.

'I don't want to put you to any trouble for dinner, tonight, Melanie,' he went on when she came over to pick up the empty tray. 'I'll buy us all some Chinese takeaway.'

'Oh, goodie,' Ava said, clapping her hands delightedly.

'Yum,' Kirsty agreed.

Gemma said nothing. She'd never had Chinese takeaway. Or takeaway anything other than the hamburgers and chips she'd been given free from the café. The housekeeping money had never stretched to such luxuries. She wasn't even sure if she liked Chinese food, though she'd always liked the smells emanating from the Chinese restaurant not far from the café she'd worked in.

'Not for me, Nathan, thank you,' Melanie said. 'I'm going to visit my brother and his family tonight for dinner.' Everyone watched as she carried the tray from the room with a quiet dignity. Gemma was beginning to admire her more and more.

'Then it's just the four of us,' Nathan said, smiling as his eyes travelled around the remaining three women to finally land—and stay—on Gemma. 'Do you like Chinese food?'

She found his gentle tone and direct gaze both disarming and disturbing. God, she hoped she wasn't blushing. 'I . . . I'm sure I will.'

He blinked disbelief at her. 'You've never had Chinese food before?'

Her laughter was self-conscious. 'I think, if I stay here long enough, you'll find out I haven't had a lot of things before.'

'Really.' Those lazy grey eyes glittered with dry amusement. 'I'll look forward to introducing you, then, to all those delights as yet untasted.'

Gemma stared at him. Was he laughing at her naïveté? Surely, he couldn't mean . . . No, no, he couldn't. *Could he*? Heat zoomed into her cheeks. 'I'm sure you'll find my reactions quite amusing,' she retorted, feeling flushed and flustered.

'Amusing?' His laugh was low and dark, seemingly vibrating with hidden meaning. 'Oh, no . . . not amusing. Refreshingly different, perhaps. And delightful, I'm sure. Our Gemma is delightful, isn't she, Ava?'

'Most assuredly.'

'Oh, my God, I just remembered!' Kirsty squealed and jumped to her feet. 'Dad hasn't seen my room yet.' She hurdled Gemma and grabbed her father's hand, dragging him out of his chair. 'Come on, Dad. Come on, Gemma.'

'Oh, no, you go ahead,' Gemma said, her attentions refocusing on her breasts once again. If her nipples were anything to go by, Nathan's cryptic comments had excited, rather than appalled her. Dear God, if he ever made a move on her would she have the strength to resist? 'I... I'll stay here and help Ava put this Monopoly away.'

'No, don't put it away,' Nathan called back over his shoulder. 'I'll challenge you all to a game this afternoon. I've given up the idea of writing anything this weekend.'

'Fantastic!' Kirsty exclaimed happily.

Gemma tried not to groan. She wondered if she could dash up and change without it looking odd. Yes, she would have to. She simply would. She could drag on a sweater of some sort. She would say she was getting cold.

'Gemma...'

'Yes, Ava?'

'I'm sorry if I upset you over what I said about your father being a jewel-thief.'

'But you didn't!'

'I must have. I can see it in your face.'

Gemma had to laugh. What Ava was seeing was concern over her swollen breasts and nipples. 'I'm not upset, Ava. But I am cold.'

'Cold?' She was clearly amazed.

'I'm from Lightning Ridge, remember? Anything under thirty-five is chilly. I won't be a sec.'

She dashed away.

What a pity Nathan and Kirsty had made slow progress up the stairs. They were just strolling along the corridor when Gemma, after taking the stairs two at a time, careered around the corner, her breasts in full voluptuous sway beneath her thin white top.

She saw Nathan turn, saw the direction of his eyes. She immediately skidded to a halt, but the rapid expulsion of air from her lungs did not help the situation.

'So you decided to join us after all,' he said with a cool composure she could only envy. 'I'm so glad. I've a feeling I'm going to need support once I enter this chamber of darkness.'

Kirsty laughed by his side. 'Chamber of darkness? What funny things you say, Dad. It's a gorgeous room!'

And she flung open the door. 'Enter all who dare.' And she stood back against the door to wave her father inside.

'Shall we dare, Gemma?' he said, walking over to link arms with her before she could stop him.

'I don't think you're going to give me a choice,' she returned, a slight tremor in her voice.

'No,' he said, his tone as hard as his narrow-eyed gaze. 'I don't think I am.'

CHAPTER ELEVEN

GEMMA would never have believed she could be so grateful to Kirsty's room.

'Good God!' Nathan exclaimed on entering, his arm slipping out of Gemma's as his handsome and horrified face surveyed the walls.

'What do you think, Dad?' Kirsty asked, giggling.

'It's ghastly,' he said, and threw Gemma a reproving look. She didn't mind. Reproving looks were a welcome change from hard sexy ones, and shocked exclamations infinitely preferable to muttered comments which sounded suspiciously like sexual threats.

'Mum thought so too,' Kirsty agreed happily.

'Melanie let you do this?' he directed more at Gemma than his daughter.

'She even helped,' Gemma told him.

'Good God,' he repeated.

'Don't get your knickers in a knot, Dad,' Kirsty reassured blithely. 'The posters come off the walls easily enough, which is just as well. I can take them all home with me when I go.'

He swung round at this. 'Oh? You planning on deserting the ship already?'

'I might . . . after the Easter break. Gemma will be going to work by then and Pops is sure to be home. You know what he's like with teenage girls. He drove poor Jade out of the house.'

'Only after Jade drove poor Byron right up the wall!' her father countered caustically. 'That girl would try the patience of a saint. And for your information, madam, Jade left this house of her own accord. As for *your* going home...I think your mother might need a little more peace and quiet before you inflict *this* on her.' His hand made a sweeping gesture around the room, encompassing the eye-popping walls and bed.

'Nah. Mum misses me. I can tell. She misses you too, Dad,' Kirsty added, a catch in her voice.

'Let's not get into one of those arguments again, Kirsty. It's a no-win situation. Unlike Monopoly,' he swept on, his momentary grimness replaced by a teasing grin. 'I aim to whip your butt this afternoon, madam.'

'You and whose army?' Kirsty laughed, and ran from the room. Her father dashed after her.

'Coming, Gemma?' he threw back over his shoulder.

'I'll be with you shortly,' she hedged. 'I have to get something from my room.'

Five minutes later, with her traitorous body enveloped in a huge grey sloppy Joe, Gemma went down to the living-room where Nathan and Kirsty and Ava were all ready to play. Melanie had opted out since she had to leave mid-afternoon for her visit to her family. Gemma did her best to concentrate on the game, but after a while, whenever it wasn't her turn to throw the dice, her mind started drifting to thoughts of Nathan.

Was he still in love with his ex-wife? she puzzled. He'd certainly spoken of her with care and consideration up in Kirsty's room, and clearly been frustrated when Kirsty said her mother missed him. Gemma had wondered more than once since seeing Nathan kissing Lenore in the billiard-room if they were still sleeping with each other.

Probably not, she now decided, since he was showing such a sexual interest in *her*. Gemma might have allowed her own feelings for him full rein, if everyone hadn't warned her about him. First there had been Ma, then Jade, then Melanie. Even Kirsty's recurring theme that her father was still in love with her mother was a type of warning.

She didn't want to become involved with a man still in love with his ex-wife, whose only feelings for her were lust. The thought that Nathan would try to seduce her merely for sexual gratification brought such a stab of pain to her heart that she was shocked. Could she still be naïve enough to be falling in love with him? Dear God, she hoped not. She'd been doing her best all week to behave like a good, sensible girl. She'd heeded all warnings, kept out of his way and avoided staring when he came into the room.

Till today...

Today she'd stared at him again like an infatuated idiot, making him hotly aware of how attractive she found him, making her own body respond in a way she'd never felt before. But she could not deny there was a fierce underlying excitement in the feel of her flesh all aroused and a-tingle beneath her clothes.

She'd seen a video movie once where a man had sucked at a woman's breast. She'd found it repulsive at the time, thinking that the woman could not possibly have been enjoying such an activity. Now, she knew it would probably be very exciting.

'Your turn, Gemma.'

Her eyes gradually focused through the haze her thinking had evoked to find Nathan looking at her closely. Her heart, she realised, was racing madly, her lips parted slightly to let her softly panting breaths escape. His eyes fastened on those lips before lifting to narrow on her wide, unblinking gaze. It was impossible to look away, impossible to stop the heat that accompanied the mental image of Nathan bent over her bare breasts, taking one of the aching tips deep into those beautifully shaped lips of his.

His smile was slow, his voice wry. 'The dice, Gemma.'

She gulped then threw the dice, flustered with herself and furious with him. He knew. Maybe not exactly what she was thinking, but that she had been thinking of him, thinking of him and sex.

He had no right to know what she was thinking, she stormed internally, anger her only salvation from total shame. With agitated movements she hopped her token along the board on to Mayfair, which was not only owned by Nathan but had two hotels on it.

Her groan echoed a lot of things.

'Methinks Madam Smith here is in a spot of trouble,' Nathan drawled.

Gemma refused to look at him, bending her head to start counting out the remainder of her money.

'You haven't got enough money to pay him,' Kirsty said with the satisfaction of a child glad to see one more opposing player go bankrupt. Ava had already gone broke and was merely watching.

'Never mind, Gemma,' Ava said sympathetically. 'You can help me make afternoon tea.'

'What a good idea!' Gemma plonked all her money and properties down in front of Nathan and jumped to her feet.

By the time they returned with a pot of tea and plate of biscuits, Kirsty and Nathan were in the throes of Nathan's death rattle. Good, Gemma thought vengefully when she saw he couldn't possibly win. Finally, he surrendered and started helping Kirsty pack the game away.

'I might pop down to the hospital to visit Byron,' he commented over tea. 'What time do you folks want Chinese tonight? Seven-thirty do?'

'Yes,' Ava agreed. 'That way we'll be finished before the Sunday night movie comes on. There's quite a good one tonight. *Double Trouble.* Have you seen it, Gemma?'

'No, I don't think so. I—er—haven't seen all that many movies, actually. We didn't have a television at home.' And going to the movies was expensive.

'Didn't have a TV?' Kirsty gaped at her.

'Don't get me wrong,' Gemma explained. 'I saw plenty of TV over the years at school and at friends' houses. And there was one on the wall of the café I worked in, but Dad and I lived rather—er—roughly, out in the opal fields. In a dugout, actually.'

'A dugout?' Ava looked perplexed. 'You mean you lived in a hole in the ground?'

'In a way. It was dug out of the side of a hill.'

'How big was it, Gemma?' Nathan enquired, looking genuinely interested.

'Not big at all. One large room about twenty by ten, I guess. One end was the kitchen, the middle was where we ate, and our beds were down the other end.'

'But didn't you have your own rooms and bathroom?' Kirsty asked, still looking horrified.

Gemma smiled. 'Afraid not. We had a pit toilet in a wooden shed outside, and a water tank with a sort of shower rigged up under it. When it failed to rain we collected artesian water in drums and filled the tank that way.'

Gemma gradually realised they were all staring at her as if she was a little green man from Mars. Nathan's face was the first to change from shock to admiration. Gemma tried not to respond to his admiring look but she found it impossible to stop the wave of melting warmth that flooded through her under his appreciative gaze.

God, but this was more weakening than his desire, she realised, for it left her totally defenceless and quite limp. If he touched her now, she would definitely dissolve into mush.

Fortunately, that couldn't happen at the moment. Gemma vowed to always keep people around her when Nathan was home, and soon, with a bit of luck, this infernal infatuation would die a natural death.

'I don't know how you stood it,' Ava said, awe in her voice.

Gemma shrugged, the action feeling oddly heavy. 'I didn't know any different, then later you get used to it. You can get used to anything after a while.'

'I can't imagine any of the females I know ever getting used to living in such primitive conditions,' Nathan said testily. 'Maybe you'll appreciate what you have more now, madam,' he directed at Kirsty.

She pulled a face at him. 'You always have to turn everything into a lecture.'

'True. Which reminds me, time for your homework.'

'I should get back to my painting too, I suppose,' Ava sighed.

'And I have some ironing to do,' Gemma said, standing up. No way was she going to stay here so that Nathan could suggest she accompany him to the hospital. Not only did she not want to encounter the intimidating Byron again so soon, but the thought of being alone in a car with Nathan was highly unnerving.

'*Ironing*?' Nathan's frown was dark. 'What ironing? We have a lady comes in to do the ironing.'

'Not mine,' she countered crisply. 'I'll do my own ironing, thank you. *And* my own washing.'

'Then you can do it some other time. Come with me to the hospital. I'm sure Byron would like to meet you.'

'Oh, but I met him yesterday,' she quickly prevaricated. 'Lenore took Kirsty and me to visit him, didn't she, Kirsty?'

'Sure did, Dad, and Pops is still the biggest bossy-boots in the entire world. Heaven help us when he comes home here. When is he coming home here, by the way?'

'Next Friday, I think.'

Kirsty groaned. 'Can we go to Avoca with you next weekend, then?'

'If you like...' His eyes slid slowly across to Gemma. 'You probably haven't seen the sea, Gemma, have you?'

'No...no.'

'Gosh!' Kirsty exclaimed. 'How exciting to be able to show someone something like the sea for the first time. I can't wait!'

'Oh, but I...'

'Can't wait either, I'll warrant,' he finished for her, his eyes and voice firm. 'You'll love the sea, Gemma. And you'll love Avoca. I guarantee it.'

His steady gaze held hers a moment longer than necessary before he turned away to begin striding purposefully from the room. When Kirsty ran after her father, asking him to pick up something for her from home while he was on the road, Gemma wasn't really listening. She

was, instead, staring after Nathan with a throat and
tongue suddenly gone dry.

Gemma kept telling herself that he couldn't have, in
that moment, made up his mind to show her something
far more intimate than the sea up at Avoca. No man
could be that presumptuous or that arrogantly confident of his own sex appeal, she reasoned agitatedly. No
man could be that . . . wicked.

For it was wicked to deliberately plan a seduction,
wasn't it? Wicked for a man of his age and experience to
take advantage of a young girl's infatuation. Wicked to
make her want him to do just that.

Totally besieged now by moral confusion, Gemma's
mind turned to the down-to-earth advice Ma had given
her in the letter she'd received on Friday in answer to *her*
hurried, worried letter posted the previous Tuesday.
She'd penned in a dripping Biro:

I did warn you about them city men, didn't I, love?
They can be powerfully attractive, especially the rich
handsome ones. But they don't marry poor little misses
from Lightning Ridge. Go to bed with him if you must,
love, by all means, but keep that loving heart of yours
firmly in your chest and don't forget the condoms!

But would she keep her heart firmly in her chest if she
allowed Nathan to make love to her? He only had to look
at her and the blood started rushing around her body like
a cyclist pedalling furiously round one of those circular
tracks. Round and round they went, faster and faster, till
they had to be as giddy as she was feeling.

Suddenly, Gemma realised she was standing in the living-room all alone. Sighing, she turned to walk out
through the enormous kitchen and down the corridor to
the equally enormous laundry area, complete with automatic washers and driers and a sewing-machine and
ironing-boards all set up. The first time she'd seen this
set-up, Gemma had been struck dumb, but it was amazing how quickly one got used to luxuries, amazing how
quickly one became corrupted by money.

And other things...

Nathan's return from the hospital showed a totally different Nathan from the one who'd left Belleview a couple of hours previously. He was taciturn and preoccupied, snapping at Kirsty when she complained he'd forgotten to pick up the book she'd asked him to get from her mother.

'You'll just have to do without,' he said sharply. 'I'll get it tomorrow on my way home from work.'

'What about when you go to pick up the Chinese food? Mum's place is only a couple of miles down the road.'

His jaw clenched down hard. 'Kirsty. Can you or can you *not* do without this book tomorrow?'

'I suppose I can do without it,' she muttered irritably. 'But you'd better write me a note saying why I haven't got it with me!'

'My pleasure.' And he stalked off.

'Brother, what's got into him?' she complained to both Gemma and Ava. The three girls had regathered in the family-room, which had the biggest television Gemma had ever seen, not to mention lovely comfortable squashy sofas just made to curl up in. It was the most casual room in the house—*and* the most modern—with one totally glass wall overlooking the pool and tennis court. At the moment, however, the vertical blinds were drawn, shutting out the view and the never-ending rain.

'He's probably in a bad mood because he's suffering writer's block,' Ava suggested.

'Yeah, that's probably it,' Kirsty concurred. 'Writers! Never marry a writer, Gemma. They're impossible!'

'Maybe Mr Whitmore said something to upset him,' Gemma counter-suggested.

'Possibly,' Ava replied, 'though Nathan doesn't usually let Byron or anyone else for that matter get under his skin.'

'Mum gets under his skin,' Kirsty volunteered. 'She can get him mad as a hatter. There again, that's only natural. He's still in love with her.'

'Kirsty, dear,' Ava said with a sigh in her voice, 'you really must start accepting that your mother and father are no longer in love. You're lucky they've remained such good friends. Some divorces are very bitter. But their marriage is over. There won't be any reconciliation.'

'Fat lot you know!' Kirsty jumped to her feet, face flushed, green eyes glistening. 'They're going to get back together again. I know they are. Soon as Mum gets lonely she'll come and beg Dad to go back and we'll be a family again. You just wait and see. You're just jealous because you've never had a man at all, let alone a family of your own, and you want everyone to be as miserable and lonely as you are!'

So saying, Kirsty burst into tears and ran from the room. Gemma was torn between going after the noisily distraught Kirsty or staying with the silently distraught Ava. Finally, she stayed with Ava, because the poor darling looked so crushed.

'I'm so sorry, Ava,' she apologised for Kirsty. 'She didn't mean it, you know. Especially that last part...'

Ava nodded, her face pale and sad. 'She's a very mixed-up little girl. But she's wrong, about a lot of things...'

'What things?' Gemma probed gently.

'About her father for one. He's not in love with Lenore. He's *never* been in love with Lenore.'

Gemma blinked her shock at this remark.

'Nathan's incapable of loving like that,' Ava stated with chilling certainty. 'According to Byron, who knows him far better than anyone, Nathan was so damaged by his mother's irrational and destructive behaviour that he simply refuses to relate to any woman on an emotional level. Oh, he makes a charming dinner guest, and, from what I've gathered, a stunning lover. But as someone to have a close relationship with, he's an abject failure. That's why Lenore divorced him. She wanted more than he could give. Naturally, Kirsty isn't old enough to appreciate the finer points of what makes a marriage work.'

'What...what did his mother do to him?' Gemma asked shakily.

'The woman was deplorably irresponsible! Spoilt, of course. And beautiful, naturally. She came from a very wealthy family and got into drugs when she was only a teenager. Left home at eighteen, fell pregnant with Nathan at nineteen, and generally lived a very fast life. Lots of men and parties and drug-taking. She had quite a bit of money of her own so she could support this life-style without any trouble. Nathan was only eight when she first put him into boarding-school so that she could trip around the world with her new lover.'

'Dear heaven,' Gemma murmured.

'I don't think there was too much heaven in Nathan's upbringing,' Ava said drily. 'Every time his mother was dumped by her latest lover, she'd take Nathan out of boarding-school so she would have company. Then, later on, back he would go, often to a different school. This happened so many times his formal education was a di-saster. In some ways, he was far behind the others in his class. In other ways he was far beyond them. He was al-ways a voracious reader. But he refused to cooperate, re-fused to sit exams, refused to do anything. He was expelled from so many schools, his mother actually ran out of available establishments. When he was sixteen, she managed to find one more—in a different state—but he ran away within days and came home, only to find her dead of a heroin overdose.'

'Oh, my God!'

'Byron came across Nathan a few months later at King's Cross, living a life that would have made your hair curl. Not that he told me directly. I only know as much as I do because Irene liked to gossip.'

'Was Byron a family friend? How come he adopted Nathan?'

'No. He didn't know Nathan's family at all. Byron was a founding member of a charity organisation begun in the Seventies to help street kids. He'd helped lots of trou-bled boys before but something in Nathan touched a personal chord with him and he brought him home here. I was away at school myself at the time so this is all second-hand, I'm afraid.

'As far as the adoption is concerned... Who knows why Byron adopted him? Maybe he was the son he'd never had. Irene refused to have any children after Jade was born. Whatever, by the time I came home on my next school holiday, Nathan was very much installed, with little Jade running after him everywhere like an adoring puppy. I expected Irene to object to him, since she seemed to object to everyone and everything, but Nathan was the one person she never crossed. I think she was half afraid of him. He was quite frightening in those days.'

'In what way?' She couldn't imagine Nathan being seriously frightening.

'It's hard to explain. He had a lot of surface charm and was always gorgeous to look at. Goodness,' she laughed, 'I had quite a crush on him myself for a little while. But he could look right through you sometimes. Or you could look into *his* eyes and see nothing, just a cold emptiness.' A shudder convulsed her. 'I felt sorry for Lenore when she married him. I knew he'd make a rotten husband. He had no warmth in him.'

'But he's not like that *now*!' Gemma protested, perhaps far too vehemently, for Ava looked at her with surprise in her eyes.

'He *has* improved, I admit. Kirsty improved him.'

Gemma looked away, fearful that she had betrayed too much, fearful of what her automatic defence of Nathan kept telling her.

'Gemma...' Ava began hesitantly.

Her eyes jerked back. 'Don't say it,' she snapped. 'I'm sick of people warning me against Nathan. Sick of people telling me he's bad. I don't want to hear it any more, I tell you!'

Ava blinked at her, her sweet face quite shocked now. 'I...I was only going to suggest you come upstairs with me. I've got some clothes that don't fit me any more which I think would be very pretty on you.'

A fierce flush of embarrassment invaded Gemma's cheeks. 'Oh,' she said, then, 'Oh, God.' And she dropped her face into her hands.

A silence descended on the room.

'I know you don't want me to say this, dear,' Ava said gently at last, her hand on her shoulder. 'But I feel I must, in the circumstances. I didn't realise how you felt, which was very stupid of me. Aside from anything else I've just said, Nathan's way to old for you, dear. Way too old and way too experienced and way too... too...'

When Ava couldn't finish what she wanted to say, Gemma was compelled to look up. 'Way too *what*?' she demanded to know.

'I can't seem to find the right word. But something awful happened to Nathan either while he was growing up or after his mother died, something that twisted his ideas where women are concerned. He still desires them but basically he doesn't *like* them, let alone love them. That's not the kind of man for you, Gemma. You're warm and sweet and giving and you need a man who will appreciate you, who will love you back with his whole heart and soul. Nathan is not that sort of man.'

Gemma frowned. Every instinct inside her screamed denial of what Ava was saying. You're *wrong*, she wanted to argue. Nathan can love as strongly and deeply as any other man. He just hasn't found the right woman yet.

But if Ava was wrong, then so was every other woman who knew Nathan. They were all of the same opinion. She was the only one out of step.

'I do realise, Gemma,' Ava went on sadly, 'that Nathan must seem quite a glamorous, romantic figure to a young girl like you. But please...listen to what I'm telling you. I wouldn't like to see you hurt, because I like you, dear. I like you very much.'

Gemma was almost moved to tears by her concern. 'You're very kind, Ava. I won't forget what you've said, and I will try to be careful. But I can't promise not to find Nathan attractive. It's too late for that.'

Ava tut-tutted. 'That man has bewitched every woman at Belleview at some time or other. But who knows? Maybe he'll do the decent thing *this* time,' she bit out, 'and leave you alone.'

Gemma blinked. Who was she thinking about when she said that? Who were the women Nathan *hadn't* left alone?

Melanie? Jade, perhaps? Ava herself?

Gemma's blue eyes widened when her mind eventually moved to the one woman who had lived at Belleview, till recently. Byron's dead wife...Irene...

No, no, she instinctively rejected. He couldn't have done that. He wouldn't. Not her Nathan!

It was at that precise moment that Gemma accepted she was not merely infatuated with Nathan Whitmore any more. She was totally, blindly, irrevocably, in love with him.

CHAPTER TWELVE

By the end of that week, Lenore knew she would never be cut out for the role of the 'other woman'. She and Zachary had snatched half an hour for a brief lunch together in the city on the Wednesday, but the whole time they were together she'd been in a highly nervous state, glancing around, afraid some mutual acquaintance would see them together. Yet, on the Saturday night previously at the Royal, she hadn't worried for a moment over such an occurrence.

Of course... they hadn't been illicit lovers then...

The same guilt poisoned any pleasure for her when she telephoned Zachary at his office. She'd agreed to ring him there, because she couldn't very well ring him at home and it was too awkward for him to contact her at the theatre during rehearsals. But by the third call she was sure she heard a sly, knowing tone in the secretary's voice once she gave her name. Zachary said she was imagining it, but nothing he could say soothed the ghastly squirming feeling in the pit of her stomach. She felt like a scarlet woman, a pariah, an evil scheming bitch who was trying to take a good man away from a virtuous wife and their innocent children.

Friday came and went without her calling Zachary at all. She simply hadn't been able to face the guilt. She drove home from the theatre, her spirits low, her depression deep. For she could see no happiness for herself with Zachary. Their relationship was as doomed as it had always been. One night of passion had not changed that. *Nothing* would ever change that.

She turned into her street, and there was Zachary's car, parked at the kerb. And there was Zachary behind the wheel, waiting for her, a grim look on his face. That would have been bad enough, but a glance in the rear-view mirror before she slid her own car into the driveway revealed Nathan's sleek navy blue Mercedes coming round the corner.

Lenore was almost sick on the spot.

Lurching to an unsteady halt, she sat in the car for a few seconds, her stomach churning. Not all the acting ability in the world was going to extricate her from this mess. There was nothing left but to brazen it out.

Lenore's mouth curved into a rueful smile as she climbed out of the car. Well, that was what Nathan had always thought she was. Brazen!

By the time she walked back down the driveway, Nathan had parked his car behind Zachary's and both men were standing on the pavement, facing each other like duellists at dawn. All that was missing was the pistols. Nathan caught the tail-end of Lenore's smile as he glanced over Zachary's shoulder at her and gave her a look that should have killed her at a hundred paces, pistol or no pistol.

But Lenore was used to Nathan's glares.

'I presume you've come for Kirsty's book at last,' she said with a blasé boldness that even astounded herself. 'She rang me last night to say you keep forgetting to pick it up.'

'I came by last Sunday for it,' he returned coldly, 'but you were otherwise occupied. Which reminds me...' Those cold grey eyes slid back to Zachary. 'If you intend sleeping with my ex-wife on a regular basis these days,' he said in the most insulting tone, 'then get yourself a less noticeable car. Or alternatively, go and do it in a sleazy motel room like most adulterers.'

Lenore's sharp intake of breath could be heard over the sudden stark silence. Her eyes swivelled to Zachary who, as always, won her respect and admiration with his unshakable composure under fire.

'I appreciate your concern, Nathan,' he returned just as coldly, 'but I think the operative word is *ex*-wife. Who Lenore sleeps with these days is none of your concern. She's not your wife any more.'

'Neither is she yours,' Nathan counter-attacked with the thrust of a rapier-like tongue. 'As for Lenore's moral habits not being my concern . . . then you're very much mistaken. Unfortunately, she happens to be the mother of my fourteen-year-old daughter, who you will agree is at a very vulnerable age. If her mother must screw around with another woman's husband, then I would appreciate she do so with a little more discretion.

'I will not have my daughter exposed to depravity, do you hear me?' he lashed out suddenly, stunning Lenore with the savage emotion that blazed momentarily in those normally implacable grey eyes.

But, as always, Nathan was quickly under control again, only the shrugging of his shoulders under his suit jacket showing the excruciating tension that had momentarily seized him.

'I would have thought your own sons' welfare mattered to you as much, Zachary,' he continued, his voice returning to glacial. 'Clearly, I was wrong. There again, you do have my pity. When Lenore decides she wants a man he just doesn't stand a chance. Fortunately for me, she hasn't really wanted me in years. I can only hope she grows bored with you as quickly. But I doubt she will while you're married to another woman. There's nothing so stimulating as someone society dictates you shouldn't have.'

Zachary's punch was conceived with his heart rather than his head, so that Nathan saw it coming and ducked sideways. But Zachary still landed a glancing blow on one ear. Nathan's fists clenched and flew up in defence, death in his eyes.

'No!' Lenore cried, and jumped between them, facing Nathan. 'Please don't,' she begged, tears filling her eyes. '*Please* . . .'

He stared at her for a few seconds, then frowned a bewildered frown. 'You really love him, Lenore?'

She nodded.

'And I love her,' Zachary declared, taking her by the shoulders and moving her to his side. 'We love each other.'

'You'll divorce Felicity, then?'

'No.'

'Why not?'

'I don't want to hurt her.'

Nathan's laugh was harsh and bitter. 'You think you're not hurting her now, you bloody fool?'

Nathan laughed again and whirled to leave.

'The book,' Lenore called after him. 'You've forgotten Kirsty's book.'

Nathan turned back, a mocking smile on his face. 'Now that's getting your priorities right, Lenore. Just don't forget your daughter *after* I'm gone, that's all I ask. And don't let Zachary forget *his* sons. They have feelings too, you know. The day you forget children are human beings with feelings is the day you condemn them to a living hell!'

Lenore stared at the man who had been her husband all those years and glimpsed, for the first time, the man he might have been, if he hadn't been warped and twisted by his childhood. He'd never revealed the horrors of his existence with his mother, her very basic knowledge of his upbringing coming from Ava via Byron. Whenever she'd tried to bring the subject up, he'd simply refused to discuss it, saying he preferred to forget a past that had little to recommend it in terms of the future.

Now she saw the depth of the damage, and was moved to real sympathy. Oh, Nathan... if only you'd let someone in, really in, there might be hope for you yet.

With an unhappy sigh, she turned and went to get the book. When she returned it was to find Nathan and Zachary talking quite civilly about some whizkid Byron was thinking of hiring to help him revamp Whitmore

Opals. Nathan, it seemed, was intent on returning to full-time writing once Byron was back on his feet.

'Here's the book, Nathan.'

'Thanks, Lenore. At least now Kirsty will get off my case.' He turned back to Zachary. 'I dare say Byron will be in touch. He values your advice.'

'What do you personally think?'

'I think it's time for some new blood. And it's time Byron learnt to delegate more. He can't do everything himself. It's only since I've taken the reins for him that I've realised how much he used to do. The man's a workaholic. I know he *wants* to change, but it's hard to change at his age. Hard to change at *any* age,' he added drily.

Lenore stood by, listening to this interchange with growing irritation. It never ceased to amaze her the way men could keep the various parts of their lives separate. Work was work. Home was home. Affairs were affairs. Each had its own compartment and their own emotions, with lines firmly drawn between.

Women, by comparison, were not so capable of stopping everything from overlapping. This last week had been a perfect example. Her performance at rehearsals had been pathetic. There was no other word for it. Lenore knew the director was worried and if she kept up her abysmal standard of acting he would fire her and replace her with the understudy.

But her mind had simply not been on the play...

'Lenore,' Zachary said brusquely. 'Nathan's gone. Can we go inside, please? I have to talk to you.'

Lenore blinked back to reality, knowing that Zachary had shifted gears from 'work' to 'affairs', with its accompanying shift of emotions. His polite pragmatic face of a moment ago now mirrored a grim bleakness that made her shrink back in fear. 'You...you shouldn't take too much notice of Nathan,' she tried in vain. 'He doesn't understand love.'

'He understands children,' came the bitter reply. 'And he's right about my hurting Felicity.'

'F...Felicity?'

'She knows, Lenore,' he said in a tortured voice. 'She knows...'

Nausea rose in Lenore's throat but she gulped it down and somehow made it inside where she staggered out to the kitchen and poured herself a bracing drink before facing the subject of Felicity's knowledge once more.

'You want one, Zachary?' she called out as she slopped far too much gin into a glass.

'No. I have to drive home shortly.'

She topped the gin up with ice and bitter lemon then drank quickly and deeply, returning to the living area to find Zachary pacing agitatedly up and down.

'How does she know?' she asked.

'I have no idea. Maybe I gave myself away unwittingly somehow. Maybe I was too keyed up when she came home from her sister's last Sunday night. Maybe I've been acting like a guilty man all week. Hell, Lenore, I probably did a million things wrong. I've never had an affair before. Perhaps I tried too hard to act normally with her. God knows. I don't. I thought I was playing the role of innocent husband quite well. But she's been giving me the strangest looks ever since Sunday.'

'You never mentioned this on Wednesday,' Lenore reminded him curtly.

Her sharp tone brought him to a halt. 'Do you think I'm making this up?'

She shook her head in abject misery. 'No...'

'She hasn't accused me, but a couple of times, when I came home from work, I knew she'd been crying. I've been avoiding her in bed, you see, not going upstairs till I thought she was asleep. Last night, however, she came downstairs dressed in one of her prettiest nighties, and she actually tried to be...seductive. She probably thought she was doing the right thing but Felicity has never been an aggressive woman, sexually, and I'm afraid I must have looked shocked, or something, because suddenly she turned and ran from the room. When I followed her, she was sobbing on the bed. When I tried to take her in my arms she pushed me away, saying that it was hope-less, that it wouldn't be any good anyway and she would never lower herself like that again.'

'Oh, Zachary...'

'Yes, Lenore, that's exactly how I feel. Lower than the lowest.'

'But she doesn't *know*, my darling,' she tried to soothe. 'Maybe she suspects but she doesn't really know.'

'I can't live with her suspicion, or her pain. I can't live with myself if I do to her what was done to my own mother. I can't be happy over another person's misery.'

'What...what are you trying to tell me?'

'It's over, Lenore. I won't be coming to see you any more. Don't ring me. Don't drop into the office. And don't, for God's sake, even contemplate trying to force my hand by confronting Felicity and confessing all. If you do, I'll never speak to you again as long as you live.'

Shock and hurt rooted Lenore to the spot. She could not believe Zachary would think she would do such a thing.

'Oh, don't give me that injured innocent look, Lenore. You and I both know we crossed a line last Saturday night and it will be damned difficult for either of us to step back behind that line again. I'm doing it voluntar-ily, but I'm *forcing* you to do it. So it's quite likely that you'll come out fighting once you feel the bitter corner of loneliness again. But I beg you, Lenore, don't...don't take your pain out on my family.'

'I'd never do that, Zachary,' she said brokenly. 'I promise you, I'd never do that...'

'I didn't really think you would,' came his strangled reply before hanging his head a moment, his shoulders sagging as though a huge weight had been dropped on them. 'God, Lenore, I thought it was hell before, but now...' He looked up and took a halting step towards her, then checked himself. 'If I touch you...I won't be able to go through with this...'

Tears flooded her eyes, but her chin lifted. 'Then don't touch me, Zachary.' Her voice was surprisingly steady. And quite hard.

'So be it,' he pronounced bitterly, and with rapid strides carried himself out of the room, out of the house, and out of her life once more.

'You remembered at last!' Kirsty exclaimed delightedly when Nathan handed her the book. 'Only took you a week,' she added cheekily.

Gemma refused to look up from where she was sitting at the table in the family-room, pretending to study her Japanese. Her first awareness that Nathan was standing at her shoulder was that familiar pine smell teasing her nostrils, then she glimpsed a dark grey trouser leg out of the corner of her eye.

'Say something for me in Japanese,' he said.

She looked up, surprising herself with being able to stare into that handsome face and betray not a flicker of emotion. Still, she'd been practising hard all week. Clearly, practice did make perfect, she thought, despite still being bitterly aware that her pulse-rate had quickened alarmingly.

'*O genki desu ka*?' she said.

'*Hai O Genki Desu, O genki desu ka, Gemma san*?'

She gaped at him. 'You never told me you spoke Japanese.'

He smiled, pulling out an adjacent chair to sit down at the table with her. 'Saying that I'm fine and being able to ask how a person is won't make me fit to be ambassador to Japan. But I can hold a basic conversation. Byron, however, can chat away like a native.'

'I don't think I'll ever be able to do that,' Gemma sighed.

'I'll give you a hand, if you're ever stuck.'

Gemma stiffened slightly. 'Thank you very much, but I'm sure I'll get the hang of it shortly. I've got little else to do during the day. Frankly, I'm not used to being so... useless.'

'Did she say she was being useless?' Ava called from the lounge where she was sitting, watching the television and eating chips. 'Don't you believe her, Nathan. She runs around here doing things all day. Insists on helping Melanie with the housework, bullies me into finishing my paintings, does her own lessons and homework. She even found time this past week to alter a whole lot of clothes I gave her. She makes me tired just watching her!'

Kirsty coming over to plonk down in another chair at the table was a welcome distraction. 'At least the rain has finally stopped,' she said. 'What time are we leaving for Avoca in the morning?'

'Early,' Nathan pronounced crisply.

'How early is early?' Kirsty asked.

'Six.'

'Six! I'm not even conscious at six.'

'Then stay behind. Gemma and I will go alone.'

'Not on your life! I've been looking forward to this all week. It's going to be such a ball, showing Gemma the beach and the rocks and everything. I'd get up even earlier if I had to!'

Gemma found her knuckles going white as she clenched her Biro harder and harder. She'd hoped to find some excuse all week not to go. But nothing had come to mind and now the moment was almost at hand. Seeing there was no way out of it, her only thought was to have the beach-house filled with as many people as possible.

'What about you coming too, Ava?' she suggested. 'I'm sure Nathan wouldn't mind, would you?'

This presumption on her part simply had to be accompanied by a polite glance his way, where she found to her consternation that he didn't *look* annoyed.

Yet there was something in his eyes—something watchful—that made her feel like a hunted animal who was slowly being forced into a smaller and smaller space where a net lay in waiting. Or a pit. Yes, she felt like she was balancing on the edge of a deep dark pit, where a sharp stake awaited at the bottom ready to pierce her heart.

'Yes, do come, Ava,' Nathan further surprised Gemma by saying. 'We'd love to have you. We could play Monopoly again on the Saturday night and have some more Chinese.'

'Thanks for the offer, Nathan, dear, but the beach and I are not on good terms. All that sun and sand.' She shuddered delicately. 'Besides, I don't have a swimming costume that fits me. No, I'll stay home here and keep Byron company.'

'Where is Byron, by the way?' Nathan asked Ava.

'Doing his leg exercises. He hasn't stopped since you brought him home this afternoon. The man's mad.'

'If it keeps Pops out of our hair, Ava,' Kirsty said, 'then don't complain.'

'Believe me, I won't, dear. By the way, Nathan, I've been meaning to ask, did you find out anything about Gemma's mother? I've been dying of curiosity all week.'

Gemma looked up, startled. She'd forgotten all about her mother, her mind consumed with none other than the man sitting next to her.

'The news is not good, I'm afraid,' he sighed, his voice full of sympathy. 'Your birth certificate isn't a forgery, Gemma.'

'*What*?' everyone exclaimed.

'I...I don't believe it,' Gemma rasped. 'I was sure I was older than eighteen. I was sure that was my mother in the photo.'

'You may very well be,' Nathan consoled. 'Legal does not necessarily mean accurate. Your father could still have supplied false details to the registry. In fact, it seems highly likely he did, since there is no birth, marriage or death certificate for a Mary Bell of about the right age in the whole of Australia. According to the records, your mother does not exist.'

'That's crazy!' Kirsty scoffed.

'It's also impossible,' Nathan said drily. 'So I suggest you give me that photograph you have, Gemma, and I'll have a good investigator look into it. And before you say anything, I'll pick up the tab.'

She stared at him and wished with all her heart that he didn't have some ulterior motive in doing such a thing.

'Poor Gemma,' he drawled, his hand reaching to cover hers. 'You look stressed. A couple of days relaxing up at Avoca is just what you need.'

'Same here, Dad,' Kirsty piped up with the innocence of a child. 'School has been hell this week. I hope you've got a swimming costume, Gemma. We're going to hit the beach as soon as we get there.'

'Yes, she has,' Ava answered for her. 'I gave her one I bought at a sale a couple of years ago in anticipation of my latest diet actually working. Needless to say, the poor costume has never seen the light of day.'

Kirsty gave Ava a worried look. 'What's it like? It's not—er—matronly, is it?'

Gemma almost laughed. There was nothing even remotely matronly about the shiny slinky purple maillot Ava had pressed upon her. If it hadn't had a roomy matching shirt to wear as a cover-up, she would probably never have the courage to wear it at all!

Her brown eyes stared deeply into Nathan's cool grey gaze, her throat turning dry at what she saw in its determined depths. There would be no hiding from him this weekend, she realised. Time had run out. She'd avoided him all week, keeping her eyes averted, her body under a tight control.

But the moment had come, the moment when he would take advantage of her love for him, when he would show her what she had never seen before, when he would invite her to taste the delights she had never tasted.

It was just a question of when.

CHAPTER THIRTEEN

LENORE sat in the living-room in the dark, dressed in nothing but a robe and drinking her fifth gin—or was it her sixth?—while she contemplated the future.

If Kirsty had been younger, she might have resigned herself to dedicating the rest of her life to her child. But in less than four years Kirsty would leave school and embark on her own journey through life. A smothering over-possessive mother would be the last thing her spirited stubborn daughter would want.

Which left Lenore nothing but her acting.

She sucked in then let out an emotionally exhausted sigh. Acting had lost its magic for her. Life had lost its magic for her. Without Zachary by her side, she might as well be dead.

Could one die from drinking too much gin? she wondered fuzzily. It would be good if you could. What a way to go! People made jokes about men who had heart attacks while having sex, but Lenore thought passing away in a haze of gin was infinitely preferable.

She stood up unsteadily and went to pour herself another, but most of the gin missed the glass.

'I'm drunk,' she told the ice-cube tray just before she dropped it. 'Damn,' she muttered and was trying to rescue the slippery cubes from the kitchen floor when someone rang the doorbell.

Lenore muttered another less ladylike word, abandoned the ice-cubes and weaved her way to the door.

'Who ish it?' she called out. Even drunk, she wasn't a fool. It was ten o'clock at night and one didn't simply open one's door without knowing who was on the other side. 'If it's you, Nathan, get loshed.'

'It's me, Lenore. Zachary.'

'Z...Zachary?'

Fumbling, Lenore opened the door and promptly burst into tears. Zachary stepped inside, closed the door and gathered her in.

'Oh, Zachary, Zachary,' she sobbed, clinging wildly and pressing moist kisses to his neck. 'You came back... You came back...'

Suddenly, she pushed him away and slapped him hard, around the face. 'You barshtard!'

By this time, Lenore's emotional state was very fragile indeed. She was crying, angry, confused, despairing.

'Lenore,' Zachary said firmly, taking both of her hands in his. 'You're drunk.'

As if to underline this, she hiccuped.

'I'll put some coffee on,' he said, 'and before you give me any more trouble, you crazy adorable woman, then let me tell you that I'm not a bastard. I haven't come back here simply to go to bed with you again, although I won't say no to that...eventually. But because everything is going to be all right.'

She gulped. 'All...right?'

'Yes. *All right*. Felicity and I have agreed to a divorce, though for Clark's sake we've also agreed to keep it under our hats till he's finished his HSC.'

'A divorce...' Lenore's knees went from under her. Zachary scooped her up and laid her gently down on the sofa, tenderly pushing her hair back from her face and bending to kiss her several times on the lips.

'You...you wouldn't lie to an intoxicated person, would you, Zachary?' she whispered shakily.

'That depends,' he smiled, and bent to kiss her one more time. 'Must be gin. I can't taste a thing.'

'Don't tease.'

'With you? I wouldn't dare.' He stood up, still smiling. 'You just lie there and sober up while I get you some coffee.'

'Zachary, no!' She reached out her right hand, desperate fingers imploring him to come back to her. 'Don't go. I'm fine. Come back and sit beside me. Tell me what happened.'

He did as she asked, leaning over and kissing her once more before straightening. 'Very well. I'll start from the moment I arrived home after leaving you earlier this evening. I have to admit I was very distraught after our—er—parting, and had not managed to get myself entirely under control, so that when I walked in to find Felicity in floods of tears I was not at my most patient.'

'What did you do?' Lenore asked, finding it hard to picture Zachary losing his temper with Felicity.

'I guess I exploded. God, Lenore. I'd just made the most monumental sacrifice for that woman and there she was, weeping and looking at me like I was a monster or something worse. I...I demanded to know what was wrong with her. Guilt and rage made me totally irrational. I ranted and raved, told her I had been the best husband a woman could ask for. I demanded to know what more she wanted of me.'

'And?'

'She broke down and confessed that she'd fallen in love with another man, had started having an affair with him and now wanted to marry him.'

Lenore sat bolt upright. 'My God, Zachary! And you never suspected?'

'Not for a second. The symptoms were there, of course, but I was so caught up with my own feelings for you, Lenore, not to mention my own guilt, that I didn't see them.'

'What symptoms? You said she was trying to *seduce* you the other night.'

'Ah, yes...the famous, or should I say now infamous seduction? You know those times she's been dashing off to see her sister?'

'Uh-huh.'

'She was seeing her lover and her sister was covering for her. Not sleeping with him, mind. Apparently that didn't happen till last Saturday night.'

Lenore's eyes widened. 'You mean the same night that we...we...'

He nodded. 'The very same. Ironic, isn't it? It seems, like me, she was so stricken with guilt by the end of the next day that she told her lover that she could never see him again and came home to try to make the best of things.'

'The poor love... But who *is* this mysterious boy-friend? Anyone you know?'

'Not at all. Apparently he met Felicity in a music shop when they were both enquiring about the same album. Felicity has always been large on music. Well, anyway they got talking, found they had a lot in common, he asked her for coffee and one thing led to another. He's a widower, apparently, with a grown family. Quite well off. Would you believe Felicity told me that she's always felt inadequate as my wife, but that Errol—that's his name, by the way—that this Errol makes her feel smart and needed? Do you know how that made *me* feel? To think I've crushed her self-esteem all these years. To think I'd made her feel...unwanted.'

Lenore said nothing because she could see some truth in Felicity's accusation. Zachary would not have meant to crush his wife's self-esteem, but he was an exception-ally clever, self-sufficient and strong-minded man. Any woman of Felicity's hothouse-flower make-up would have withered under the crushing force of his tough, slightly insensitive personality, whereas Lenore was not the easily crushable type. Besides, after Nathan's chill-ing idea of a relationship, she found Zachary positively warm and responsive.

When he continued to look bleak she leant forward and kissed him on the cheek. 'Don't start being hard on yourself, Zachary. You're a good man. The best. And don't you ever forget it.'

His smile touched her. 'You say the sweetest things sometimes.'

'Oh, go on with you. Now tell me the rest, and don't forget the bit about the night Felicity tried to seduce you.'

His smile widened. 'You would want to know about the sexy bits. Well, it seems that despite Felicity's best intentions to stick with our marriage she'd been trying to avoid having sex with me, going to bed extra early and pretending she was sound asleep when I came into the room. Another irony, considering I was staying up later and later for the very same reason. Finally, guilt got the better of her and she decided to take the bull by the horns.'

'Darling, what an evocative phrase!' Lenore said naughtily. She couldn't help it. Happiness was making her saucy and bold. Everything was going to be all *right*! 'You don't have to go on,' she said into his reproving face, all the while doing her best to keep a straight one. 'I get the picture.'

'I can see you need a strong man to keep you under control,' he rebuked.

'Am I going to get a physical demonstration of your controlling abilities?'

He groaned, sandwiching her face between trembling hands and taking her mouth in a kiss that just stopped short of an oral assault.

'Good lord!' she gasped when his head finally lifted. 'I think you'd better stop that and finish your confession before we get carried away.'

'Finish my confession?'

'You did tell Felicity about us, didn't you?'

'Yes, of course.'

'And?'

'I think she was relieved, though naturally, I didn't say I'd been in love with you all these years. That would have been cruel. I let her think I'd always found you attractive but that it wasn't till I ran into you last Saturday and asked you to go to the play with me that I realised I'd somehow fallen in love with you. I think she was so happy that I wouldn't be devastated by her own defection that she didn't stop to think we hadn't even seen each other in the last two years.'

'So we're to keep our relationship a secret till the end of the year, is that it?'

He reached out and picked up a stray curl and looped it back over her ear. 'Do you mind very much, my darling?' he said, continuing to smooth back her hair from her flushed face. 'We could go away for weekends, have discreet dinners. I could stay the night sometimes when Clark is at his friends' places, which is often. Look, I know it isn't ideal but it will come to an end and it's a small price to pay to secure everyone's happiness. Emery's mature enough to cope but Clark's desperate to be a pilot and he needs a good pass in his HSC for that. Neither Felicity nor I would be able to live with ourselves if we thought we'd somehow ruined his chances by our behaviour. Our divorce will still upset him, but once he's on his feet he's sure to be able to cope better.'

'I have a child too, Zachary,' she reminded him. 'She might be coming home to live next school term, which could put a stop to any nocturnal stayovers. I doubt Kirsty and Clark will be so co-operative as to go to friends' places on the same nights,' she finished a touch curtly before realising she was being both stroppy and selfish.

What was the matter with her? She'd gone fifteen years without Zachary at all! What did one miserable year of small sacrifices matter in the long run? It wasn't as though they wouldn't be able to see each other at all. Where there was a will there was a way!

Smiling softly, she smoothed the frown from his face with gentle hands, her lips following her fingers. 'I'm sorry,' she apologised. 'I'm being silly and selfish... We'll work it out... Oh, I do so love you, Zachary...' She kissed him full on the mouth.

He quickly took control of the kiss, pushing her back on the sofa and effortlessly reducing her to a trembling mess. She lay there in a daze of desire when he stood up and started tossing his clothes aside like a sex-crazed adolescent. His last sock flung aside, he bent over to reef the sash on her ivory silk robe undone, pushing the material roughly aside. When he ran his hands quite roughly down her quivering nakedness she arched her body in response and gave a voluptuous shudder.

'Women like you should be prohibited,' he groaned, and, without any further foreplay, joined her on the sofa and fused his flesh with hers. 'I don't think this is going to be one of my better demonstrations of my controlling abilities,' he rasped on setting up a desperate driving rhythm.

'Mmm,' was all Lenore could manage before tumbling headfirst into a wildly shuddering climax which precipitated Zachary's release even earlier than he'd anticipated.

After the storm had passed, they lay together in blissful peace, Zachary having pulled Lenore on top of him so that they could fit more comfortably on the sofa. He was happily playing with her back and buttocks under her silk robe, which slithered around their nakedness with a whispery sensuousness.

'Talk to me,' he said softly.

Lenore's head lifted. '*Talk* to you?'

He stroked her head back down on to his bare, hairroughened chest. 'Yes, talk to me, tell me everything about yourself that you've never had a chance to tell me. I want to know it all, warts and all. I want to know what you were like when you were a little girl, I want to know when you decided to become an actress, I want to know... oh, I want to know the damned lot. Hey!' He suddenly jerked upwards and stared down his very damp chest. 'You're crying!'

Cupping her face, he stared into her blurred eyes, his own bewildered. 'What did I say wrong? What did I do wrong?'

'Nothing,' she sobbed. 'You do everything so right that I can't stop crying with happiness.'

'God, you had me worried for a second,' Zachary said. 'I'm not used to a woman crying with happiness. I'm not used to a woman lying naked with me on a sofa, either,' he added thickly, a slight lift of his hips making Lenore hotly aware that things were on the move in his nether region. 'Do you—er—think we might leave our deep and meaningful discussion for just a few minutes?'

Lenore wiped her eyes, laughed and sat up.

'Now that's better,' Zachary growled. Then a few seconds later, 'God, yes, that's definitely better. Oh, you gorgeous beautiful wild creature... I do so love you...'

CHAPTER FOURTEEN

GEMMA didn't wait for seats to be assigned in Nathan's Mercedes the following morning. She immediately climbed in the back and belted up, leaving Kirsty happily to occupy the front passenger seat. Nathan made no comment on the arrangement, though his eyes did meet Gemma's in the rear-view mirror as he went to reverse out of the garage, and their expression suggested a dark amusement over her actions. She quickly tore her eyes away, annoyed to find her heart was beating madly.

A look, she thought despairingly. One miserable look...

'Well, we're almost away on time,' Kirsty said brightly. The clock built into the dashboard showed six twenty-five.

The dark blue sedan swung back in an arc once free of the huge garage door—it was a six-car garage—Nathan closing the door by remote control before he guided the car along the side-path and on to the circular drive which would lead them round to the front gates.

'Good God, Dad!' Kirsty burst out. 'That's Jade's car, isn't it? Look where she's parked it. It's almost in the fish pond!'

And sure enough, the white sports car Gemma had seen the day she arrived at Belleview had its bumper bar over the edge of the pond surrounds, skid marks on the grass where its driver had careered across the front lawn before coming to a precarious halt.

Nathan braked and just glared at the car. Everything about his very still body suggested sheer fury.

'I hope she'll still be here when we get back,' Kirsty added. 'Jade's fun.'

Nathan threw her a withering look. 'You've got a funny idea of fun, then, madam,' he ground out. 'If she's thinking of staying any longer than a day or two, then you'll be going back to your mother faster then the Bluebird crossed Lake Eyre. I'm not having you anywhere near that crazy female on a permanent basis.'

'Oh, Dad!' Kirsty wailed.

'What the hell's she doing back here anyway? She's got her own damned place up at Avalon now. Why doesn't she stay in it?'

'Maybe she's come home to visit her father,' Gemma suggested quietly from the back seat.

Kirsty spluttered into hysterics and Nathan muttered something marginal.

'I take it Jade doesn't get along with Byron?' Gemma asked, curious now.

'You take it correctly,' was Nathan's very dry comment, and continued driving round towards the gates, which were already opening.

'Why not?'

'To put it bluntly, she and he have different moral standards. He can't abide hers and she can't abide his.'

'In regard to what?'

'I don't think I care to discuss this any further right at this moment,' he said stiffly, and, turning the car into the main street, accelerated away with a sudden burst of speed.

'Oh, Dad, don't be silly,' Kirsty said in that bored tone teenagers liked to adopt when patronising their parents. 'I already know all there is to know about Jade. What Mum hasn't told me, Ava has. She's man-mad, Gemma. That's all. Dear old Pops just can't handle his little princess always having the hots for a different guy every week. She's not bad, she's just kinda wild and groovy!'

'Kirsty!' her father reproved. 'Does your mother let you go around talking like that?'

Kirsty shrugged. 'What did I say that was so bad?'

Nathan sighed. 'For one thing it is not healthy to be man-mad. Aside from the moral angle, it's downright dangerous. What if Jade ends up with AIDS? Have you thought of that?'

'She won't end up with AIDS, Dad. She's too smart.'

'Good God,' he muttered irritably. 'Can you talk some sense to her, Gemma? Maybe she'll listen to you.'

'I think what your father is trying to say, Kirsty,' Gemma said carefully, 'is that there is no fool-proof protection for the risk involved in having casual sex with a lot of different partners.'

'What about condoms?'

'They minimise the risk,' Nathan rejoined the discussion. 'They don't eliminate it. And who's to say a girl like Jade will always be in a fit state to think of protection? She drinks like a fish. And she's already been arrested once for possession of drugs.'

'Oh, Dad, it was only grass. That's nothing nowadays!'

'That comment perfectly demonstrates your immaturity, my girl, in matters of drugs as well as sex. Do you think people go to bed one night and wake up a heroin addict? They have to start somewhere and it pretty well always starts with marijuana. So don't understate its corrupting powers.' He slid a sharp glance over his daughter's way. 'You haven't been experimenting with drugs, have you?'

'Of course not!' Kirsty denied, but she was also blushing fiercely.

'You'd better not be. You're not too old to be taken over my knee and given a good paddle on the backside, and I'll do just that if I find you've been so foolish. Gemma, has Kirsty said or done anything to make you think she might be taking drugs?'

'No, Nathan, she hasn't.'

'Just as well.'

'*See*!' Kirsty pouted.

'Yes, I do see,' her father said very seriously. 'I see, and have seen, far more than you'll ever see!'

A tense, brooding silence descended on the car during which Gemma realised that not once in that brief discussion about Jade had her mother been mentioned. It was almost as though she had never had a mother, yet Irene had only been dead a few weeks. It was all very puzzling. But she supposed she would find out all about the Whitmore family over the coming weeks if Ava kept up her level of gossiping. That woman never shut up. Privately, Gemma thought she was a very lonely soul, filling her life with meaningless chatter and little else. Which was a pity, because Gemma believed she had real talent as a painter. Her watercolours were quite lovely, and would be even lovelier if she ever finished them!

It was hard, too, to think unkindly about Ava who'd so sweetly given her all those lovely clothes. Admittedly, most had still been slightly too large, though not the cream linen bermuda shorts she was wearing, nor the purple silk shirt that she'd teamed with it.

Thinking about Jade and Ava must have passed quite a bit of time for suddenly Gemma saw they'd left the suburbs far behind and were flying along a busy multi-laned highway with little on either side except stark, scrub-covered hills through which the road had been cut with bold disregard for the rocky terrain. A railway line followed a similar route, with Nathan's powerful car streaking ahead of the occasional silver train they momentarily drew parallel with.

The atmosphere in the Mercedes remained silent and slightly strained till the road angled down a steep incline and they burst on to a big bridge which crossed the most beautiful stretch of water Gemma had ever seen.

'Oh, how lovely,' she gasped in delight, swivelling her head from one side to the other. She didn't know which view she preferred. On the left, the river curved magnificently into the distance, an island in the middle, houses dotting the shore. Or on the right, where more than one vista boggled her eyes. Straight ahead, the already wide river grew even wider into a hugely impressive body of water, more islands and another bridge in the distance.

But if she twisted around she could see the cutest little bay, full of boats, a tiny village hugging the hills that rose up behind.

'I've never seen such a pretty place,' she admired. 'Or such a beautiful river!'

'It's the Hawkesbury,' Nathan informed her. 'And that's Brooklyn you're looking at back there, where all the boats are moored. You can hire cruisers or houseboats down there for trips up the river. You can go for a day, or a weekend, or longer, if you wish.'

'Can you? Oh, I'd love to do that one day!'

'Then we will.' Again he caught her eye in the rearview mirror and this time, he was smiling at her without any hidden mockery or sardonic knowingness. Gemma felt a rush of such pure joy that tears pricked at her eyes, tears of the sharpest happiness. They blurred her vision slightly but she could not look away, and in that moment of bittersweet pleasure, that moment of mutual enjoyment, she pushed aside all her fears where this man was concerned.

He couldn't mean her any harm, she decided. He couldn't possibly be bad. Not the man who'd comforted her so kindly out at Lightning Ridge. Not the man who'd so generously looked after her since her arrival in Sydney. Not the man who obviously cared so deeply for the moral welfare of his daughter.

Such a man could not be a callous seducer.

The ice and her fears broken, the rest of the trip to Avoca was happy and cheerful, Kirsty busily pointing out the various spots of interest while Nathan concentrated on the driving. Despite their early start, the freeway was very busy in Gemma's opinion, though she was told the traffic was light for a summer weekend.

'That's where you turn off to go to Old Sydney Town.' Kirsty prattled away, rarely expecting an answer, though Gemma did get to pop in a comment or a question occasionally. 'It's like a living museum of the olden days... We'll have to take Gemma there one day, Dad... And now we're going down the hill to Gosford... Isn't it a

pretty town...? There's the League's Club... That big
sheet of water? It's called the Brisbane Water, though
God knows why, we're a long way from Brisbane... Yes,
it's very green up this way, and the bush is real thick...
High rainfall, isn't that right, Dad?... Sorta like a rain-
forest... Listen to the bell-birds...some bloke wrote a
poem about them once... Dad will probably read it to
you some time...he's a poem and play nut...a book nut
too... Mrs Danvers? Never heard of her... Who's Mrs
Danvers, Dad?'

'A housekeeper in a book called *Rebecca*. The house
was called Manderley.'

'Who was Rebecca?' Gemma asked.

'The master of Manderley's first wife. She died mys-
teriously but was so powerful a personality that when the
master married a second time—to a quiet, shy girl—his
new wife felt her marriage was haunted by the memory
of the first wife. The housekeeper, Mrs Danvers, loved
Rebecca and hated the second wife. She made her life
hell.'

Gemma shuddered. 'Poor thing.'

'I've got a copy of the book at the beach-house. You
can read it if you like.'

'She hasn't come up here to read, Dad. She's going to
go to the beach with me!'

'Not all day, she isn't. She'll get burnt.'

'Gemma? Burnt? She's already got a fantastic tan.'

'The sun at the beach can be very deceiving. It reflects
off the sand, doubling the exposure. And we don't have
an umbrella.'

'Just as well,' Kirsty said. 'I wouldn't be seen dead using an umbrella!'

'You might be dead in a few years if you don't start
using one. Haven't you been listening to the ads on television about skin cancer?'

'Oh, not another lecture, Dad. I couldn't stand it.'

Nathan laughed, then grinned in the mirror at Gemma.
'Shall we give her a reprieve for the weekend?'

'Only if she promises to wear the sunscreen I bought yesterday.'

'Done!' Kirsty agreed. 'Anything but the dreaded umbrella. Oh, look, we're here! The sea is over there, to the left, Gemma. It's a bit hard to see from the road but you can just glimpse it occasionally between the buildings and the trees. Slow right down to a crawl, Dad. Now you can see it!'

Gemma looked left where Kirsty was pointing across a park. 'It's so blue!' she exclaimed.

'And very rough,' Nathan added ruefully. 'No walking round the rocks today, Kirsty. And before you object, remember what happened to those poor people last year.'

'What happened?' Gemma asked.

'A family of foreign tourists were up here on holidays and couldn't read the warning signs. There's a very interesting walk around the rocks, you see, near the base of the cliffs, which on normal days is quite safe, but when the tide is high and the sea's whipped up by a strong wind the waves crash over the rocks. Mostly, that isn't really dangerous either, if you're not standing too close to the edge, but every now and then a big wave comes that takes people by surprise and washes them into the sea.'

'What happened to the family?'

'They drowned. Mother, father, and two children.'

'Dear God . . . You won't get me going on those rocks, then, even in calm weather.'

'I'll take you when it's safe,' Nathan offered.

By this time they'd driven slowly past a funny old barn-like building which Kirsty astonished Gemma by pointing out as the local picture theatre. It looked like something out of the ark, more fitting to Lightning Ridge than the tourist mecca of the Central Coast.

She laughed her astonishment.

'Don't laugh. It's real interesting inside, isn't it, Dad, with all sorts of quaint old posters and pictures? It's not as bad as it looks, either. There's air-conditioning and free tea and coffee and on top of that, it's real cheap.'

'The seats are a bit hard on the derrière after a while,' Nathan admitted, 'but the kids love it. On Saturday nights in the summer, it has an all-night session.'

'Which I haven't been allowed to go to so far,' Kirsty pointed out drily.

'Maybe this year, if you've got someone to go with you. And don't look at me. My days of going to the pictures on a Saturday night with a mob of noisy teenagers are long gone.'

Kirsty twisted round and gave Gemma a hopeful look.

'Don't look at me either,' she laughed. 'I can't stay awake after ten-thirty.'

'Maybe Cathy's up here with her parents...' Kirsty frowned, then brightened. 'I'll find someone, never you fear. I'm not going to let a chance like this go by.'

Nathan groaned. 'Me and my big mouth. Well, here we are, folks. Everyone out.'

The beach-house was not Belleview. But it wasn't Gemma's idea of a beach-house either. Weren't they supposed to be rough-and-ready affairs? She should have known that any family used to living in Belleview wouldn't rough it. Hadn't Nathan said as much when she'd told them about the dugout?

It was up on the side of the hill that looked down on to the antique movie-house, cream brick and split-level with a front balcony that was larger than her dugout back at Frog Hollow and a back balcony that overlooked a private pool. The block was bounded by tall thick trees on three sides, giving them privacy from the neighbours while not impeding the magnificent view of the Pacific Ocean. Though not air-conditioned, each room had its own ceiling fans. The décor was modern and casual, with polished floors, cane furniture and assorted rugs for warmth and comfort. The kitchen was a dream and there were two bathrooms, three if you counted the shower and toilet downstairs near the pool.

Gemma finally shut her gaping mouth, trying not to shake her head as she wandered out on to the front decking a second time. If only Ma could see her now! Fancy clothes. Fancy cars. Fancy houses.

Glancing down over the railing, she spotted Nathan as he strode down the steep driveway and round to the back of the car again to collect a second load of luggage. He was wearing crisp bone-coloured canvas jeans and a caramel-coloured shirt which had an open collar neck and a sailboat logo on its single breast pocket. Sometime since arriving he'd slipped on a pair of expensive-looking sunglasses, the effect being to make him seem even more glamorous to her than ever.

A wistful sigh escaped her lips and she turned to walk back through the sliding doors into the large living area.

'Come on, Gemma,' Kirsty called out as she dashed down the hallway that led to the bedrooms. 'Get your cossie on. There's not a moment to waste. I have to get down to that beach and find someone to go with me to the movies tonight.'

Gemma walked down to stand in the doorway of the room Kirsty was proceeding to turn from tidiness into a tip. Clothes were being pulled out of her bag and thrown everywhere.

'Don't tell me I've forgotten my own cossie. Oh, there it is!' she sighed, and glanced up. 'Shake a leg, Gemma. Oh, you're waiting for your luggage, I suppose. Still, don't wait for Dad to come with us. He might pop down later but he's sure to hole up in his den, writing for the next few hours.'

'Are you bad-mouthing me again, young lady?' Nathan growled from just behind Gemma's shoulder.

'Who, me?'

'Yes, you. I've put your things in your room, Gemma. By the way, there's plenty of beach towels in the linen press and if you're hungry the kitchen is kept well stocked. You look after Gemma, Kirsty. But you're right, I probably won't be down the beach till later. I have things to do.'

Gemma watched him walk down the hall and disappear into the furthest room which she'd peeped into only a minute or two before. It was clearly the room he wrote in, a combination of study, library, office and sitting-room. It was the only room in the house Gemma hadn't liked. The windows were covered with heavy curtains which blocked out the natural light and gave the room a dark claustrophobic feel. It had been cold in there too. She recalled shivering a little and quickly shutting the door.

The door shut behind Nathan with a definite click.

'Well, that takes care of Dad for today,' Kirsty grinned. 'Come on, Gemma, time for your introduction to the wide blue Pacific!'

CHAPTER FIFTEEN

GEMMA hated the sea. Well, not exactly *hated* it. But it frightened her, especially when she waded in and felt its power, pushing her towards the shore on top and sucking her back out underneath. Kirsty kept telling her it was extra rough that day, that the waves were all horrible dumpers, that there was an awful rip and that she shouldn't judge on this first unfortunate meeting, but Gemma knew she would never like placing herself at its mercy. The die had been cast.

In the end she begged off staying and Kirsty walked her back to the house where they made some toasted sandwiches, Gemma having a cup of tea while Kirsty drank a couple of the long-life milk drinks in the fridge. They each polished off an ice-cream from the freezer before Kirsty announced she was going back to the beach in search of some other starters for the movie marathon that night. The aforementioned Cathy had been found, but they were both keen to gather a large group.

'Why don't you read that book Dad was telling us about? *Rachel*, wasn't it?'

'No, *Rebecca*.'

'Yeah, that's the one. I'll go ask him where it is.'

'Do... do you think you should interrupt him?'

'Probably not. But if I don't, he'll forget to eat.'

Nathan emerged from the den with a scowl on his face and frustration in his body language. Finding the book in the book-shelves in the general living area, he tossed it on the kitchen counter and was striding back down the corridor when Gemma asked him if he'd like her to make him some lunch.

He swung round, that tight, tense look still in his eyes. She held her breath, aware that though the purple shirt was covering her costume from neck to thigh the buttons weren't done up and the gap between the free-falling sides revealed not only her substantial cleavage but the highly cut purple V between her thighs. When his eyes travelled from her face down her scantily clad body to focus on this spot, a wave of embarrassing heat swept right through her like a flash flood, making her suck in a startled breath. Suddenly, her throat felt as if it had been scraped with sandpaper.

His voice sounded raw too, when it came. 'It can't be lunchtime yet, surely.'

'Well and truly,' Kirsty informed him, fortunately not having witnessed their searing visual exchange. She'd walked out on to the balcony to hang the wet towels over the railing, coming back in time to hear his comment about the time. 'It's one-thirty.'

'Good God,' he muttered.

'The writing going well, I take it?' Kirsty teased.

'No, it bloody well isn't,' he snarled.

'Tch tch, Dad. Such language.'

'Why don't you do something useful like help Gemma make me some lunch, there's a good girl?'

'Oh, Gemma won't mind doing that by herself. I've got to go back down the beach. See yuh!' She was waving and tripping off out the door and down the front steps before Gemma could drag some air into her bursting lungs.

She looked at Nathan, eyes wide. He looked at her, eyes narrow.

Not a word was spoken. Not a breath breathed.

Slowly, and almost resignedly, she imagined, he moved towards her, grey eyes darkened to slate, one of those appalling smiles tugging at his gorgeous mouth.

'I thought I told you not to look at me like that,' he said at last, his right hand reaching to tip up her chin, his gaze dropping to her softly parted lips. His smile faded as his thumb rubbed over her bottom lip. 'You should have listened to me...'

That tantalising hand drifted down the column of her throat, moving closer and closer to her aching, straining breasts with their aching, straining nipples.

'I'm sorry I wasn't able to give you good news about your mother,' he said, his matter-of-fact tone mocking what was happening between them. 'I was as surprised as you were that that birth certificate was legit. I could have sworn you were more than eighteen. Or maybe I just wanted you to be. Do you really want me to take it further, make more enquiries?'

She blinked up at him, baffled by his choice of conversation. How could he coolly talk about her mother and her age while his hands were tracing the curves of her breast, stroking the undersides, moving closer and closer to those tight aching tips pressing hard against the Lycra?

Somehow, she managed to nod a blank assent, her head feeling terribly heavy, her eyelashes drooping. Yet when his fingertips finally reached and brushed over her nipples, her head jerked upright as though she'd been stung. Wide brown eyes lanced his and she had the satisfaction of seeing that he was no longer looking so cool or controlled.

'I've been wanting to touch you like this since that very first day,' he whispered in a voice vibrating with passion. 'You've been wanting the same thing, haven't you?'

She nodded again, her tongue thick in her mouth. She would have admitted to anything to keep those hands on her breasts, to keep him doing what he was doing.

His eyes narrowed till they were dark slits of the most incredible desire. 'God, but you're the loveliest thing I've ever seen,' he rasped, and, parting the shirt further, he pushed it back from her shoulders, dragging it down her arms and letting it flutter away to the floor.

'You're a virgin, aren't you?' he asked, and peeled the costume down to her waist, baring her breasts to his smouldering gaze.

She swallowed, and nodded again.

Maybe if he'd groped or pawed her, memories from that other experience might have risen to spoil things, bringing revulsion and fear. But his touch was so incred-

ibly light and sensual that her mind was soon filled with
nothing but the most heavenly haze.

Yes, run your fingertips over them again. Yes, mould
your hands around them like that again. Yes, oh, yes,
please kiss them...

A startled gasp fluttered from her parted lips when he
did, and she swayed backwards. He caught her, lifted her
and carried her down the hall and into his bedroom, lay-
ing her on the double bed and stripping her naked with
firm but gentle hands. She watched, dazed, while he removed his own clothes, stunned by his smooth golden
beauty, awed by the power of his desire.

Her head reeled when she felt his nude hard body cover
hers, pressing her down into the mattress. His expression intense, he stroked back her dark hair on to the white
pillows, then held her face and finally, finally, kissed her
full on the mouth.

It was everything and more than she could have
dreamt, bringing with it a dazzling explosion of desire
that had her lips opening wide, inviting the most intimate of kisses. His groan as he filled her with his tongue
was as arousing as the kiss itself, making her twist rest-
lessly beneath him, making her wind her arms around his
back and scrape his skin, ever so lightly, with her nails.

He broke off the kiss, his breathing heavy. Once more
she felt the thrill of his lips on her breasts, though this
time they were not so gentle. There was no more tender
licking. He suckled at her like a greedy infant, drawing
her nipples deep into his mouth, grazing them with impassioned teeth then tonguing them to an excruciating
level of sensitivity.

A sigh of ragged relief burst from her lips when he
abandoned her breasts to slide further down her body,
burying his face in the softness of her stomach. Gemma
was astonished at how sensual it felt to have her navel
licked, and it was while she was marvelling at this highly
erotic experience that his hand slid between her thighs.

From that moment on, she was delirious with pleasure. Oh, God, yes, she thought. Yes, please. Oh, don't
stop. Oh, please, don't stop. Oh, God...

'Oh!' she cried aloud, and shuddered convulsively when her body was racked by a series of the sharpest, most electric spasms. But just as suddenly it was over, and a draining exhaustion washed through her, leaving her limp and heavy.

When she sighed, he immediately retreated and she was left experiencing a bewildering emotion that both puzzled and upset her. There was peace, yet emptiness. Satisfaction, yet resentment. This was not how it was meant to be, surely?

Her eyelids fluttered open from where she'd been squeezing them tightly shut only to find Nathan stretched out beside her on the bed, his chest rising and falling as he dragged in a series of deep, shuddering breaths.

'Nathan?' she said, her voice oddly husky. She tried to lift her hand but it was heavy and languid, falling across his still heaving chest.

He picked it up and pressed it to his lips, startling her back to sexual awareness by sucking one of her fingers into his mouth. When her head rolled sideways on the pillow to stare at him, he shocked her even further by taking her hand and carrying it down his body till he enclosed her fingers intimately around him. With his hand still imprisoning hers, he forced her to caress him, pressing her fingers tight, making her squeeze as well as stroke.

He groaned with a raw animal pleasure and with the sound of his own mindless pleasure any hint of revulsion vanished from Gemma. She became enthralled, her head spinning with the intoxication of sexual power, her mind thrilling to the way she could make him shudder and cry out. Soon, his hand dropped away from hers and he lay there gasping as she propelled him to a climax that left him shaking uncontrollably.

'God,' he muttered, and, shuddering one last time, rolled off the bed and strode into the *en suite*, shutting the door firmly behind him. There came the sounds of a tap running, then a cupboard opening and closing.

Gemma lay there, feeling suddenly awkward and embarrassed, but within seconds the bathroom door was reefed open and Nathan was back on the bed with her, slipping something under the pillow then gathering her back in to the warmth and security of his arms.

'Sorry about that,' he said ruefully. 'But it's some time since I've been with a woman, and I wouldn't have lasted long enough inside you to give you a hope of satisfaction.' His eyes glittered as they looked deeply into hers. 'Inside you... good God, even saying those words is enough to turn me on again.'

And it was, her eyes rounding as she felt his desire rubbing hard against her thigh.

'Don't worry,' he said. 'I keep a good supply of condoms in the medicine cabinet.'

Now her eyes widened further and he laughed softly. 'There's no obligation on our part to use them all. But I think one is definitely in order.'

She watched, half curious, half shy, as he retrieved a small plastic envelope from under the pillow and, with obviously expert fingers, extracted then drew on the seemingly inadequate protection. In no time he was back, cupping her face and kissing her hungrily. 'Now I can love you properly, my darling. I can concentrate on giving *you* pleasure, beautiful unselfish gorgeous sexy creature that you are.'

Gemma was dazzled by his words, by his calling her his darling, by his overwhelmingly confident sexuality. There were no fumbling moves, no furtive actions, no feeble excuses for what he'd done earlier. He'd had a plan in mind and he'd executed it boldly.

'I don't think you know how irresistible you are,' he went on. 'How you've tormented me these past two weeks. I tried to put you out of mind, but I see now that was an insane solution to what you've done to me. There is only one solution. Only one...'

He was kissing her again, and the explorations of that erotic, demanding tongue excited her unbearably. Soon, she was writhing beneath him, panting and pressing her flesh into his, her lush, nubile young body arching upwards in a driving need for closer contact. When he slid down her body to suckle her breast, her arousal flared to frustration. She moaned, shaking her head from side to side on the pillow.

'No,' she cried huskily. This was not what she wanted. She wanted what *he* wanted. Him, inside her. 'Do it,' she urged. 'Just do it!'

His head lifted. 'Patience,' he exhorted gently. 'I don't want to hurt you.'

'I don't care if you do,' she insisted wildly.

His smile was dark. 'Oh, yes, you would... if I did. Now just lie here and be still,' he ordered, 'and leave this up to me.'

Be still! Was he mad? She wanted to move, to... to touch him, to...

She froze. For he had slipped a pillow under her buttocks and was pushing her knees right up, opening her body to his gaze. Her face flamed and she might have shut her legs but already he was between her thighs and God, he was rubbing himself against her and...and...it felt so heavenly, so *glorious* that any protest, verbal or physical, died in her suddenly dry throat.

Gemma swallowed, closed her eyes and gave herself up to what was happening to her. And once she surrendered the last shreds of her defences, her mind spiralled out into a dark erotic wasteland from which there seemed to be no returning.

'Yes,' she moaned in agreement when he stopped the increasingly frustrating rubbing to probe the velvet depths of her stunningly aroused flesh. Only a shallow penetration at first, but steadily more and more, till he was filling her completely.

'Oh, yes,' she groaned, and blindly reached out her arms for him.

He came to her. They clung together, and for a few seconds Gemma was overwhelmed by a feeling of intense emotional love. But when Nathan braced his body with his elbows on either side of her and started a deep and powerful rhythm she was spun back into that wasteland, where nothing existed but a black haze and what was happening deep inside her.

There was a gathering of heat and tension and pleasure that wasn't really pleasure. It was a yearning, a
longing where everything twisted tighter and tighter, and
only seconds before she thought she must surely disinte-
grate she did, her flesh shattering around his in a series
of stunning sensations that scorned her first climax as
nothing but a sip at the cup from which she was now
drinking her fill.

'Oh, Nathan,' she cried out beneath his own shuddering body. 'I love you so much.'

Finally, he collapsed upon her and they clutched at
each other, gasping and still trembling with the ebb-tide
of their pleasure. Gradually their breathing quietened and
Nathan left her to make a brief visit to the bathroom.
When he came back to lie down beside her on his back,
thoughtful grey eyes on the ceiling, a quite appalling silence descended on the room and Gemma suddenly
found herself down in that pit, that stake through her
heart.

He doesn't love you, you fool, came the cruel voice of
reality. He's one of those handsome city devils Ma
warned you about. He wanted you and now he's had you.
End of story.

'Gemma . . .' he said at long last, sounding worried.

'It's all right,' she rushed in. 'I . . . I shouldn't have said
I loved you. It was silly. I don't expect anything from
you. I know you couldn't possibly be in love with me. I
understand. You still love Lenore and . . .'

His head and shoulders shot up then, his eyes stunned
as he turned to her. 'Lenore!' he exclaimed. 'I don't love
Lenore. Good God, whatever made you think such a
stupid thing?' Abruptly, he dragged her into his arms.
'It's you I want, you silly little ninny. Why do you think
I haven't been able to write? You've been obsessing my
mind and my body. All I can think about is having you,
and God forgive me, I'm going to.'

'You . . . you are?'

'Yes, damn it, I am,' he muttered. 'I'm going to have
you in my bed every night, and at my breakfast table
every morning, and in my life every damned day.'

Abruptly, he rolled over and pulled her on top of him. 'Gemma,' he said with steely eyes.

'Yes?'

'We're going to be married. As soon as possible.'

Gemma could not believe what she was hearing.

'You . . . you can't be serious.'

'I am. Deadly serious. What's the matter? Don't you want to marry me?'

'Yes, of course, it's what I want more than anything in the world, but . . . but what is everyone going to say?'

'A lot, I would imagine. But we won't tell them till it's a *fait accompli*.'

'Nathan, I . . . I'm not sure that—'

He pulled her mouth down on his. 'Just say yes,' he growled a minute later. 'Just say yes and let me worry about the rest.'

She just said yes and he kissed her again, and soon her head was back in the clouds. Nathan loved her and wanted to marry her. He didn't love Lenore. He wasn't a callous seducer. He was her hero, her Prince Charming who promised to fix all her problems.

It all seemed a little incredible.

But as he carried her further into the abyss of ecstasy, Gemma became blissfully certain that she would be happy with Nathan for the rest of her life. He filled her mind and her heart and her body. In the end, nothing else mattered, not the possible problems back at Belleview, or her lost heritage, or even the mysterious black opal that had first propelled her into Nathan's life. They were trivial and insignificant at that moment. They were consigned either to the past or the far distant future. All that mattered for her was the moment, and the moment was, indeed, miraculous.

She sighed, and surrendered to its pleasure.

FLYAWAY VACATION SWEEPSTAKES!

This month's destination:

Glamorous LAS VEGAS!

Are you the lucky person who will win a free trip to Las Vegas? Think how much fun it would be to visit world-famous casinos... to see star-studded shows...to enjoy round-the-clock action in the city that never sleeps!

The facing page contains two Official Entry Coupons, as does each of the other books you received this shipment. Complete and return all the entry coupons— **the more times you enter, the better your chances of winning!**

Then keep your fingers crossed, because you'll find out by August 15, 1995 if you're the winner! If you are, here's what you'll get:

- Round-trip airfare for two to exciting Las Vegas!
- 4 days/3 nights at a fabulous first-class hotel!
- $500.00 pocket money for meals and entertainment!

Remember: The more times you enter, the better your chances of winning!*

*NO PURCHASE OR OBLIGATION TO CONTINUE BEING A SUBSCRIBER NECESSARY TO ENTER. SEE REVERSE SIDE OF ANY ENTRY COUPON FOR ALTERNATIVE MEANS OF ENTRY.

FLYAWAY VACATION
SWEEPSTAKES

OFFICIAL ENTRY COUPON

This entry must be received by: JULY 30, 1995
This month's winner will be notified by: AUGUST 15, 1995
Trip must be taken between: SEPTEMBER 30, 1995-SEPTEMBER 30, 1996

YES, I want to win a vacation for two in Las Vegas. I understand the prize includes round-trip airfare, first-class hotel and $500.00 spending money. Please let me know if I'm the winner!

Name_____

Address _____ Apt. _____

City   State/Prov.   Zip/Postal Code

Account #_____

Return entry with invoice in reply envelope.

© 1995 HARLEQUIN ENTERPRISES LTD.   CLV KAL

OFFICIAL RULES

FLYAWAY VACATION SWEEPSTAKES 3449

NO PURCHASE OR OBLIGATION NECESSARY

Three Harlequin Reader Service 1995 shipments will contain respectively, coupons for entry into three different prize drawings, one for a trip for two to San Francisco, another for a trip for two to Las Vegas and the third for a trip for two to Orlando, Florida. To enter any drawing using an Entry Coupon, simply complete and mail according to directions.

There is no obligation to continue using the Reader Service to enter and be eligible for any prize drawing. You may also enter any drawing by hand printing the words "Flyaway Vacation," your name and address on a 3"x5" card and the destination of the prize you wish that entry to be considered for (i.e., San Francisco trip, Las Vegas trip or Orlando trip). Send your 3"x5" entries via first-class mail (limit: one entry per envelope) to: Flyaway Vacation Sweepstakes 3449, c/o Prize Destination you wish that entry to be considered for, P.O. Box 1315, Buffalo, NY 14269-1315, USA or P.O. Box 610, Fort Erie, Ontario L2A 5X3, Canada.

To be eligible for the San Francisco trip, entries must be received by 5/30/95; for the Las Vegas trip, 7/30/95; and for the Orlando trip, 9/30/95.

Winners will be determined in random drawings conducted under the supervision of D.L. Blair, Inc., an independent judging organization whose decisions are final, from among all eligible entries received for that drawing. San Francisco trip prize includes round-trip airfare for two, 4-day/3-night weekend accommodations at a first-class hotel, and $500 in cash (trip must be taken between 7/30/95—7/30/96, approximate prize value—$3,500); Las Vegas trip includes round-trip airfare for two, 4-day/3-night weekend accommodations at a first-class hotel, and $500 in cash (trip must be taken between 9/30/95—9/30/96, approximate prize value—$3,500); Orlando trip includes round-trip airfare for two, 4-day/3-night weekend accommodations at a first-class hotel, and $500 in cash (trip must be taken between 11/30/95—11/30/96, approximate prize value—$3,500). All travelers must sign and return a Release of Liability prior to travel. Hotel accommodations and flights are subject to accommodation and schedule availability. Sweepstakes open to residents of the U.S. (except Puerto Rico) and Canada, 18 years of age or older. Employees and immediate family members of Harlequin Enterprises, Ltd., D.L. Blair, Inc., their affiliates, subsidiaries and all other agencies, entities and persons connected with the use, marketing or conduct of this sweepstakes are not eligible. Odds of winning a prize are dependent upon the number of eligible entries received for that drawing. Prize drawing and winner notification for each drawing will occur no later than 15 days after deadline for entry eligibility for that drawing. Limit: one prize to an individual, family or organization. All applicable laws and regulations apply. Sweepstakes offer void wherever prohibited by law. Any litigation within the province of Quebec respecting the conduct and awarding of the prizes in this sweepstakes must be submitted to the Regies des loteries et Courses du Quebec. In order to win a prize, residents of Canada will be required to correctly answer a time-limited arithmetical skill-testing question. Value of prizes are in U.S. currency.

Winners will be obligated to sign and return an Affidavit of Eligibility within 30 days of notification. In the event of noncompliance within this time period, prize may not be awarded. If any prize or prize notification is returned as undeliverable, that prize will not be awarded. By acceptance of a prize, winner consents to use of his/her name, photograph or other likeness for purposes of advertising, trade and promotion on behalf of Harlequin Enterprises, Ltd., without further compensation, unless prohibited by law.

For the names of prizewinners (available after 12/31/95), send a self-addressed, stamped envelope to: Flyaway Vacation Sweepstakes 3449 Winners, P.O. Box 4200, Blair, NE 68009.

RVC KAL